Remember

By: Preston Lingle

For those I love, and will love.

Chapter 1

-Crawling In The Dark; Hoobastank-

Darkness. That's all there was. Pure and complete darkness. Nothing stirred, nothing talked, nothing happened at all. It was just a blank, empty being of nothingness. Nothing entered, nothing left, nothing returned. Then from out of the darkness, something emitted a light. A light that shined so bright, it illuminated the darkness, and formed objects when the light shined upon them. A man stood in the darkness, grasping a flashlight with the clenched fingers of his hand.

The man was indistinguishable, as the darkness only created a silhouette of him; formed from the light that his flashlight emitted, and reflected upon to him. He shone the light from his flashlight all about the darkness, trying to get a feel for his whereabouts. To his left there was a chain-link fence. Inside of the fence, he could see a slide, a swing set and some children toys littered around some mulch, as well as a few benches; all without color. They were all just silhouettes of what they should be. The slide looked to be a bit crooked, as the placement of the plastic slide looked to be tilted to one side; the man couldn't distinguish what side it was turned to. The swings stood still and didn't move, for there was no wind or any force in which to speak of that could move them. The benches had lumps on top of their shadowed figure, most likely crumbs of food or toys that were left behind. The man thought to himself, *"Must be a park..."*

The man then switched his attention from the park on his left to the undiscovered area to his right. He shone the light over in that direction to see what could be in store for him. He noticed cars; cars as far as the eye (flashlight) could see. They all looked to be very close to the ground, and very sleek. The cars, in addition to everything else in this world, were also coated with a heavy shade of black which enveloped everything about the cars. The light being emitted from the flashlight seemed to bounce off the cars, as if they had a sense of shininess to them. Pointing the flashlight toward the darkened sky, the man read a sign, which read, "Dave Sinclair FORD".   The man thought to himself, *"Huh…never heard of Dave Sinclair before…maybe it's an out-of-town dealership? If that's the case, then that only begs the question…where am I…?"* The dealership was lifeless; nothing moved, and cars just sat there—occupying space. There was something else unsettling about the dealership, too, the man thought. It was eerie to him; like something could come out and alter his life forever at any given moment.

The man took the light off the sign and pointed the flashlight forward, or, at least, in front of his body. It seemed to be a highway that looked to never end. Miles and miles it could go on; not a car in sight, though. Not off to the sides, or on the road itself. *"Well, at least no one is driving…"* he thought, seeing as that may be for his best interest.

Curious as to what this place is, or better yet where the man was, he shined his ray of light onto the park again, to see if there was a sign indicating the park name, or the place in which the park was located. A map, possibly, could even have been supplied somewhere relative the park if he searched around for one. That was the short-termed intention of the silhouetted man.

As he focused the light to his left, he found that the light didn't reflect off anything. He didn't see the silhouette of a chain-link fence, nor one for the slides, swings, mulch, or children's toys he saw just but moments ago. What remained was just earth. *"Is it even earth? Could it be concrete? Asphalt?"* Questions started to race though the man's mind, as he franticly took the light away from the non-existent park, and shined it onto the Ford parking lot. Much like the park, it was no longer existent. What remained looked to be like the park's remnants, bumpy ground that seemed to resemble either Earth, concrete or asphalt.

The man was, and reasonably so, spooked. Not thinking about what might have become of the highway he saw (he assumed it would just look like the park and the parking lot), he took a step toward the parking lot, and was halted by the sound of a loud, "CRACK!" The man looked down, and shined his flashlight onto the surface, on which he was standing. He saw the light reflect off the surface as he saw a reflection of himself from the ground. His reflection showed his face blackened out, like the rest of this world he was in. The rest of his body also was shrouded in darkness. The floor was made of a glass-like material, or so he assumed. Accidentally, he shifted his body weight, and the floor made a loud, "CRACK!" noise once again. The man's movements froze. He breathed in and out slowly, as if there were a gargantuan beast lurking around in the shadows. There might have been, for all he knew. After all, nothing else seemed to be making any sense in this world of darkness. Why not add a giant monster to come and eat him?

The man, trying not to shift his weight anymore, slowly moved the flashlight in the darkness, trying to see if any of the landmarks he once saw were still there. His findings, however, came up short. After a few seconds of stand-off between the man and the darkness, the man accidentally shifted his weight, be it slightly, and the floor gave in and collapsed beneath his feet. Gravity kicked in as he fell, along with the shattered pieces of the glass-like floor. Remarkably, however, the pieces of glass didn't scathe him as they probably should have.

Upon the first few moments of the man's descent, his flashlight flickered out. The man desperately shook the flashlight, hoping to rejuvenate the batteries, even if for a few more seconds. After the longest 10 seconds of this man's life, the batteries started to have a pulse again, and light flowed from the tip of the flashlight once more. Without thinking, he pointed the light beneath him, to see if there was a floor in which he would be meeting soon. There was; maybe a little less than 100 feet away, at most. It looked to be the same material as both the park and the parking lot, he noticed, and a few spectrums of light were bounced back from the glass already on the ground. The man saw color in this darkened world for the first time, and undoubtedly his apparent last. The man, knowing that there was no hope in trying to evade the enviable, closed his eyes and embraced for the impact...

Brent woke up.

Chapter 2

-Misery Business; Paramore-

Brent awoke to his heavy breathing. He noticed his body was very warm, as well. He sat in the comfort of his bed for a few seconds, trying to collect his thoughts on what just happened. After becoming conscious enough to figure out who he was, and where he was, Brent noticed there was a little bit of light showing through his curtains, which covered the windows in his bedroom. Brent then concluded that he must have been having a dream; no, a nightmare. Next, he saw that his bed sheets were saturated in sweat. Also, but not to his surprise, the pajamas he wore the previous night were also stained in sweat.

He removed his hands from under the covers, and noticed they, too, were drenched. He used his sweat-soaked hands to remove the covers from his sweaty body, as he got up and dragged his half-awake form to the bathroom, located conveniently in his bedroom. The door was unlocked and opened, as he pushed open the door with very little effort. Brent managed to find the light switch and turned on the light, illuminating the room. Grasping for the counter, Brent pulled himself up to consider the mirror.

Brent studied himself through the reflection. He looked upon his forehead, as it glistened from the sweat that covered his body. His hair was colored brown, and looked as if he was just a part of a tornado. Hair was stuck in multiple directions, with help from the sweat beading from his forehead keeping the messy hair in place. His blue colored eyes looked back at him, as he looked at the area around his eyeballs. His eye sockets had little purple bags underneath them, most likely from the nightmare which he had just awakened from. His skin color, white, but with a little tan to it, helped outline the effect. His eyes shifted from his forehead to his clothing. A blue sleep shirt, with white horizontal lines bisecting the blue, and sleep pants of the same accord were sticking to his body from the sweat covering his body.

Brent, after concluding that he looked like he just got out of a salty pool, turned on the sink faucet and splashed cold water on his face. The water made Brent cognizant, and no longer half-asleep. As the water dripped from his face, Brent reached around, blindly, for a hand towel. To be honest, Brent didn't quite think this plan through all the way. Luckily, and in short enough time, Brent finally found a towel, through vigorous amounts of hand wavering, and dried off the area around his face. Brent opened his eyes, and again looked at his sweaty body. He started to come up with a plan of how to dry himself of the salty water that covered him.

He didn't want to take a shower, seeing as he is a runner and was about to run anyway, but didn't want to walk downstairs into the kitchen, where people may see him all sweaty, and he was in no mood for questions. So, Brent, in the end, settled with stripping off his clothes, turning on the ceiling fan, and, "drying himself out."

After stripping down into his tidy-whities, Brent locked his bedroom door and turned on the ceiling fan, which hung right above his bed, to the medium setting. Brent then went over to the window, located to the right of his bed, and opened the curtain to let some natural light into the room. He then sat on the foot of his bed and felt the wind kick in to "dry him off."

While sitting on the edge of the bed, Brent got bored and decided to look around his room. So, he got up and started walking around, looking at all the materials he had scattered around his room. His bed sat in the middle of the room, protruding from the 12 'o-clock side of the walls. His ceiling fan hanging right above it. From there, towards the back of the room was the door, white and generic. To the front of the bed, however, the TV sat there, staring back at the person sitting in the bed. A 32-inch Plasma screen TV, with his AT&T U-Verse box connected into it, along with his PS3, which sat right of the TV's base.

On the bed's left side sat a tiny wooden nightstand. The top of the nightstand was a polished wood-looking texture, while the drawers and legs were white stained wood. On top of the nightstand was the remote for Brent's TV, a cup of water, in a South Carolina Gamecocks Tervis Tumbler, a picture of himself, mother and father when he was a young lad, a lamp, and a charging port for Brent's iPhone, which was where the iPhone was laying at the current moment. The charging port also acted as a radio and a bed-side clock. The clock read 8:15AM.

On the 3 'o-clock side of the room, a closet lay indented into the architecture of the walls. The closet had two wooden sliding doors in front of it, to make it look more natural to the room. Inside the left-side portion of the closet, lied the hamper in which would be emptied out once, maybe twice a week, to wash the clothes that lay inside.

Posters littered the room's walls, all of them bands, varying from Green Day to Fall Out Boy, to a personally signed Mindset Evolution poster. The walls were painted a very dark gold coloring, which obviously hasn't been recoated in some time. *"I should probably remind myself to repaint that sometime..."* Brent thought to himself, while looking at the coloring of the walls. He never did remember.

Starting to feel much cooler, and the sweat almost gone from his body, Brent walked over to the light switch, located next to the door, and turned off the fan. Brent picked up his clothes from the floor, threw them into the hamper and grabbed some jogging clothes out from the right side of the closet. He settled with black sweatpants and a yellow LIVESTRONG long-sleeve shirt. He also pulled out, and effectively put on, his favorite running shoes. Red Nike Frees. Brent always wore these shoes when he did his daily jogging.

Brent then walked back into the bathroom and proceeded to turn off the light, which was left on after he had left the bathroom earlier. Before turning off the light, though, he scanned the room to see if he had anything else in there he needed to go jogging. From the door, on his left was the sink and faucet. Slightly past the sink, but still on the left side of the room, was the toilet. It's just a normal old, run-of-the-mill toilet, with nothing special about it at all. Straight ahead of him was the shower, which the shower curtains were open. Lastly, he looked upon the area where the body towels were hanging, which was to the right off the room, near the shower. It wasn't a very large bathroom, maybe a 9 foot by 4-foot room, at most.

Brent decided he should probably brush his hair, considering it was standing on edge minutes ago. So, he went forward to the sink, pulled out a drawer, and dug out his brush. He brushed his hair down, and over to the left, making sure to cover his birthmark located upon the top of his head. The birthmark was shaped like a petal on a flower, but more misshaped and oblong.

After brushing his hair, Brent put the brush back where he found it, turned off the light, and closed the bathroom door. From here, Brent walked over to the window, closed the curtains, and proceeded to walk towards the door. He unlocked the door, and before opening it, remembered that he needed to bring his phone, headphones, and a sweatband. So, he walked over to the nightstand, plucked the iPhone from its charging port, and opened the drawer to find his headphones and an unused sweatband. Thankfully, both were on the top of everything else in the drawer (which contained some CDs, PS3 controllers, a few notebooks, pencils, and an envelope) since he specifically laid them out like that the previous night.

Before turning away from the nightstand, Brent looked at the picture of his mother, father, and him when he was younger for quite a while; he looked upon it as if he were appreciating some piece of art at an art museum.

Turning away from the picture, Brent stuffed the phone and headphones into his pocket, and slid the white-colored sweatband onto his wrist. He then marched to and out of the door, and into the hallway; with no idea of what was going to happen to him, or what he was to learn as the day went on. Little did he know that his adventure was soon to start.

Chapter 3

-Adrenaline; Shinedown-

Out into the hallway Brent went, as the light from the hallway blinded his eyes, but just a little. His eyes dilated to the sudden light change almost immediately. As he walked out into the hallway, he heard some chatter over to his left. He spun and saw two women having a conversation. Due to his dazed state, he didn't recognize who they were at first. He also couldn't make out what the conversation was about; thankfully he didn't have to worry long, for the two women stopped talking and focused their attention on Brent.

The two women were vastly different. There was an older woman, and a younger woman, both wearing the same blue dress which went down to almost cover their feet. The older woman was a bit stocky, and the younger woman looked to be a bit thin, and was also wearing glasses. One thing the two had in common, however, is that they weren't the tallest people you'll ever meet. Both looked to be about 5'3", compared to Brent's 5'10".

"Good morning, Mr. McIlrath," said the older of the two ladies. Her hands were at her sides, touching the dress that she was wearing. At this point, Brent realized who the two women were and greeted them:

"Oh, good morning, Mrs. Bayer," replied Brent. Brent, upon regaining his composure, recognized the two women as maids who worked in the mansion that Brent lived in. He tried to open his mouth to ask what the two girls were talking about, but the younger woman interrupted him before he could utter a syllable.

"Good morning, Mr. McIlrath," sputtered the younger woman. Her hands were clenched at the front of her dress, and her speaking was barely audible; her voice was very quiet. You could tell she was nervous about something.

"Good morning, Ms. Fisher," replied Brent. His mind was now no longer fixated on the question he was about to ask, and instead decided to be polite to the younger women. He, too, could tell that today might not be her most enthusiastic day. "Today is your second day working at the mansion, is it not?" he asked, calmly.

"Y-yes sir, I mean-Mr. McIlrath," she answered, nervously.

"It's OK, Ms. Fisher. You may call me, "sir" if you would like." Brent formed a little smile.

"No, I just, I mean I-um…" she stumbled over her own words.

"No need to be nervous, Ms. Fisher," Brent said, trying to comfort her, "It's not like I'm going to fire you just because you didn't put "Mr." before my last name!" Ms. Fisher didn't quite receive the joking as well as Brent intended. "So, uh, Ms. Fisher," Brent began, "today is your second day, you said?"

"Yes, Mr. McIlrath," she answered. Her voice was a little less nervous-sounding.

"So how are you faring so far?" he asked. She didn't answer; she just stared at the red and gold carpet of the top floor of Brent's mansion. Brent looked at Mrs. Bayer for an answer.

"She's doing fine. A little shaky and slow, obviously, but it was her first day," the elder woman answered. Brent then looked back at the younger lady, and got down on a knee.

"Listen, Ms. Fisher, there are certain people whom which I see potential to do great things. Now, I don't want to sound corny, but one of them is you," the young lady looked up from the floor and at Brent now, "Mrs. Bayer here is one of my most valued workers here at the mansion, so if I pair you up with her, so you can learn the ropes, then that means I trust that you can do great things. Not only here in at the mansion, but also outside of here, as well." Ms. Fisher smiled, and blushed a little in doing so.

"Well, thank you for the encouraging speech, Mr. McIlrath," she looked back at Mrs. Bayer as Brent began to get up. She was giving her the hand motion to speed it up, "but I think Mrs. Bayer wants me to go back to work with her right now."

"Yeah, well, I should go too," Brent added, "You wouldn't know this from yesterday, since you showed up later in the day because of college, but I jog every morning from 8:30AM to 9:30AM. If I'm having a bad day, then I get back around 10:00AM, or so. Conversely, on a good day I get back at about 9:15AM, or so. Oh, wait that reminds me, what time is it?" Mrs. Bayer started to unravel her sleeves of her dress to check her watch, which was complimentary of the job. Brent stopped her, though.

"Op-op-op." Brent put his hand out, flat, to motion a stop signal. "I want Ms. Fisher to give me the time." Mrs. Bayer, looking betrayed, rolled her sleeve back down, folded her arms and pouted. She was very sarcastic sometimes...

"The time is 8:35AM, Mr. McIlrath," replied Ms. Fisher, as a worried expression came across her face, since the news she just received from Brent said that he started running at 8:30AM.

"Aw, crap, I'm late! Well, you two have fun. Bye!" Brent said, as he darted off in the other direction. Down the stairs, turn left, down some more stairs, and Brent was now in the main lobby of his mansion. The floor now turned from the red and gold carpet to a silver-ish tint that covered the tiles of the main lobby. The tiles reflected Brent's movements as he carefully walked over the tiles. They were just waxed not too long ago, since he held a big party for his workers, their friends, and some of Brent's friends a few days back; Brent did not like the thought of tripping on the waxed floor and breaking his back. Brent, however, is very impatient and has hated walking slow on this tile since it was waxed. He keeps telling himself, *"Slow and steady wins the race...slow and steady wins the race..."* It's worked for him thus far, but it may also be because there's no one in the way in which he could hurt while he's been walking out of the front door the past few days.

Slowly but surely, Brent finally reached the small carpeting, in which the front door has sitting in front of it. It's supposed to be used for wiping your shoes off when it's raining, or when some other material is stuck to the bottom of your shoes, but Brent used it today for footing against the slippery floor. After reaching the carpet, Brent repositioned himself in a much more comfortable position as he opened the doors and walked outside to greet the cold, untouched air.

Upon opening the doors to the outside, the cool air smacked him as he trudged to open the door fully. It wasn't a heavy door, mind you; it was just windy as all hell that morning. *"Great...just great...it's probably about 30 degrees this morning and it's windy, to boot. Awesome..."* Brent thought to himself. Accepting that fact, he immersed his entire body to the cold of the outside, and shut the door behind him. The door slammed on its own, due to the wind.

While outside, Brent looked toward the sky. Only a few clouds could be seen in the sky that day. It was a beautiful day, perfect for a quick run. Brent then quickly scanned the driveway to his mansion. He saw the little "cul-de-sac" which, in the middle, stood a pole with an American flag hanging from it. It was being tossed around on its bounds carelessly by the wind. The "cul-de-sac", lead to a parking garage which held all the workers cars, Brent's car, and more space for other cars, if need be. Brent felt a gust of wind that cut straight through his clothing and through his body. This was his sign that he should probably start running. He then dug into his pockets and found his iPhone and headphones that he stashed earlier. He jacked in, hit shuffle on his running playlist, jumped off the stairs that led to the door, and off he went.

Brent loved running. It made him feel free; alive. It let him free his mind of all worries and just focus on what the coming turn had up ahead for him. The feeling that was created when you were breaking through the denseness of the air, creating a force of "wind" that hits your face when you run. Well today, the wind alone could do that to Brent. He didn't even have to run to feel that.

Brent went along his normal path that he follows every day. He starts from his house, and runs along the outside of the pathway that leads to a gateway, which leads him to and from his house, and then back home. Roundtrip, it's about 4 miles. And considering he can run 4 miles in an hour, sometimes even 45 minutes, he's quick on his feet. His endurance is jack, as well.

Brent is very much into Alternative/Rock music, and his music selection shows. In fact, the total amount of songs on his iPhone (and counting) is about 730. Music is a huge part of his life, and that's another reason why Brent loves to run; it gives him a chance to listen to about an hour's worth of music, while also clearing his state of mind of all worries.

The path in which Brent runs holds various sights in which to see. The first mile is a stretch of woods, littered with trees; trees as far as the eye can see. You could name any tree that appears in the Midwest, and I bet'cha it's there. It's a very lush environment, as the leaves of the trees flutter, and smack one another in the breeze; the branches of the trees stretch and flex all about to the tune that the wind creates.

At around the 1-mile mark, the environment gradually changes from a lush forest setting to a beautiful lakeside. The lake is part of a park, which has a trail that goes all-around the park, and then around the outside of one side of the lake. On Brent's property, there wasn't a fence separating the lake from the path. The lake, at some point, enters an arch of trees that, from the park, makes it look like the lake ends. On Brent's property, however, is where it continues. So far no one has ever entered Brent's property through this opening, and no one ever will. The lake also creates fog in the morning, since the sun hasn't quite radiated the air yet. Most people are annoyed by this, but Brent doesn't seem to mind it all that much. He invites the cool, wet air into his lungs while he runs. The fog generally spreads out to other parts of the path, and sometimes even touches the mansion. He's gotten used to the fog, since he runs every day on this path, and the fog never lets up.

The lakeside setting continues for about 2/3 of a mile, and then it goes back to the forest setting. Brent, personally, prefers running alongside the lake over the forest, but that may be because the lake is only visible for a short amount of time, compared to the forest. The new forest setting is much like the first mile of forest, with the only difference being that some of these trees' leaves change colors earlier in autumn than others, if at all.

In autumn, when the leaves begin to fall, Brent finds it annoying that he must compensate for the leaves that fall onto the path he runs on. It's almost like the leaves are conspiring against him, forcing him to have to either stop and brush the leaves off to the side, or just go around them, and enter the usually muddy grass that lies on the side. He's convinced the leaves have a mind of their own.

Reaching the end of the path, there is a gate which divides the road and the path leading to Brent's humble abode. It's run by a worker; whose job is much like a tollbooth worker. They monitor who's going in and/or out, and they also have a list of who can be let into the grounds of the mansion. These workers work in 6-hour shifts, so there are 4 people who work the "tollbooth" in total.

As Brent approached the gate…

"'Ello, Mr. McIlrath," said the man manning the booth. His voice had a bit of an English accent to it. He opened the window of his to booth, and put the newspaper that he was reading down on a small counter inside the booth. A small heater was also located inside of the booth. He was a tall man, but very skinny. He wore a beanie on his head, to help counter out the cold air that entered the booth every now and again. His face bore a very light beard that spread around to most of his face.

"Hello, Tollbooth Willie," said Brent, as he slowed down, and took the headphones out of his ears. He also stopped the song that was playing on his iPhone at the current moment. It was on, "Adrenaline", by Shinedown.

"You know, ma' name ain't Willie, sir. We go through this everyday…"

"I know that, I'm just giving you trouble, Mr. Nash," said Brent, half laughing, half heaving from running two miles without stopping. "Oh, hey, while I'm here, mind if I ask you something?"

"Not at all, shoot," said Mr. Nash. His head rolled down into his fist, making him look as if he's all ears.

"You seem to know everything about everyone who works at the mansion, correct?"

"Why yes, I do, Mr. McIlrath, currently 5'10", weighing 147 lbs." replied Mr. Nash, with a very sarcastic tone in his voice, and a huge grin on his face.

"What all do you know about Ms. Fisher?" asked Brent.

"Hmm? Who's tha-...oh yeah, her! She sure is a nervous creature; tiny too. Well, considering she just arrived here, I don't know much about her...yet. Why you askin'?" pondered the English man.

"Oh...no reason. She's new here, and I just wanted to know more about her, that's all..." Brent said, trying not to make eye contact with Mr. Nash.

"Uh, huh. Yeah, that's why. 'Just 'cause', you say. I think it's 'cause you like her," Mr. Nash said.

"What? Nah, I don't like her! Well, I mean I don't "like-like" her. I like her as a worker, is what I mean." Brent said, getting real defensive, and stumbling over his own words.

"Nice try, Mr. McIlrath, but I can tell when you are, 'Love Struck'! Ha-ha!" Brent just looked coldly at the worker. A big gust of wind came by, and cut through Brent's clothing. He shivered.

"Sure, is cold out this morning..." Brent said, shivering and rubbing his hands together. He was hoping he could change the subject. "Sure, wish I would have stretched before I went on my run..." Brent mumbled to himself, just quiet enough to where Mr. Nash couldn't hear him.

"I don't really notice it, ta be honest witya," Mr. Nash said, "It's all nice and cozy in my little booth. You go ahead and finish your run, don't let me bother ya. Besides, ya need to get back to your girl, eh?" Mr. Nash chuckled.

"Shut up," Brent replied, quickly. He started to pull out his headphones again. He turned the music back on, and started to put the headphones back in his ears. "So...how much do I owe ya this time, Willy? $1.25?" asked Brent, joking around. He plugged in the other headphone and began to run again.

"Ha-ha. Very clever!" yelled Mr. Nash, as Brent ran away, back through the trail, and back to his house. Mr. Nash just closed the window, sat back down and opened his newspaper to the sports section once more, awaiting the next inciting incident that his day might provide for him.

Chapter 4

-Entertainment; Rise Against-

     As Brent approached his mansion, he slowed down and eventually came to a halt as he reached the stairs before the door. He was winded, and his muscles ached from not stretching. Brent could have very easily just stretched before running, but he wasn't quite thinking right, seeing as he was off his mental schedule.

     After resting for a few moments Brent had decided to turn off his music, and start off the rest of his day. He turned on his iPhone, to turn off the sweet tunes filling his ears, and quickly looked at the time. It read 10:30AM. "Dammit! I'm really off today…" Brent thought, aloud. He then turned off his music, put his headphones into his pockets (along with the phone), wiped his forehead with his sweatband, and opened the door. The wind had died down since earlier, and the door swung open with a little less effort than before.

     When Brent took a step inside the mansion, his already warm body and the warmness of the house made Brent feel smoldering. Brent made a beeline to his room to take a quick shower, not only to refresh him, but to also get the beading sweat off him, in addition to the putrid smell that came along with it. Up the stairs, to the right, up some more stairs, and enter the first door on the left. Brent was now in his room.

     While in the room, Brent spun around and locked his door. With this done, Brent laid his phone, headphones, and sweatband onto his bed, and he undressed. He tossed his sweaty clothes into the hamper, along with the sweatband. Brent went into the bathroom, shut and locked the door, and entered the shower.

     When Brent got out of the shower, he dried himself off very thoroughly with a nearby hanging towel. He unlocked and opened the bathroom door and entered his room. He turned to his right and looked onto the closet. While deciding what to wear, he remembered that he had to go meet an old friend, Jaime Belcher, about an addition onto the mansion. Jaime was an architect, and Brent and Jaime knew each other from High School, and have (kind of) kept up on each other's lives. Brent wants to add a recreational room to the mansion, so he and his workers can have a place to decompress and maybe play a little bowling together. You know, like any normal workplace.

Brent decided upon wearing a white undershirt, a black jacket overtop the shirt, and a tie, red as fire, as well as a pair of black pants. Brent also chose to wear some dress shoes, and a fitting pair of socks for the occasion. He slipped them on very diligently, and then walked over to his bed, picked up his phone, leaving the headphones there. He then went over to his nightstand, and opened the second drawer and pulled out a few dollars that were thrown about and put them into his jacket pocket, just in case. He then grabbed his wallet, which was also located in the drawer, and slid it into the back pocket of his pants. He felt as if his wallet was safe in that pocket; every time he hasn't put his wallet in the back pocket of his pants, something bad always happens. It's just a superstition Brent has. From this, he closed the drawer, turned around, and then unlocked and opened the door to the hallway.

Brent walked from the hallway down into the main lobby. From there, Brent turned to his right and entered the kitchen area. It smelled of biscuits, sausage, bacon and eggs. As he walked in, he saw a black woman hanging over the sink, with the water running, and her hands working hastily to finish the few remaining dishes she had left to clean. Brent walked closer and said, "Good morning, Mrs. Green."

The lady put down the dish she was working on, and turned around to greet Brent. She was a stocky woman, and about normal height. She was draped in an apron that had a few stains on it, along with water marks from cleaning the dishes. Her hands were cloaked in green rubber gloves so bright that the gloves looked to be made of neon lights. Her gloves were dripping water on the floor as she began to speak with Brent. "Oh, well good morning to you too, Mr. McIlrath! Hey, where were you this morning? You weren't down here for breakfast."

"I kind of woke up late today, and I didn't want to eat really quickly, just to go run 4 miles. Sorry," Brent said, not wanting Mrs. Green to get mad at him. He looked over to the dining room, which was connected to the kitchen. A few of the chairs in the room were pulled out from the table, and the table itself was being wiped down by Ms. Fisher. She looked up, and the two made brief eye contact. Brent broke the contact, and quickly focused his attention back to Mrs. Green and her dishwashing.

"Oh, it's alright. We had plenty for all the other workers, so it doesn't matter in the end. Though I wish you hadn't skipped breakfast…it's the most important meal of the day!"

"I'm sure I'll live," Brent said, in a sarcastic tone. His stomach growled from thinking about eating. "Besides it's, what, about 11:00 now? I'm sure I can make it for another hour or two, until lunch comes around. Oh, I came down here to ask you something."

"And what might that be, sir?" queried Mrs. Green. She turned around to start washing dishes again. Brent approached her closer so she could hear his question.

"What time is my appointment to see Mr. Belcher today? I forgot."

"Ah, yes. Mr. Belcher…" Mrs. Green was silent for a few moments. "Yes, I remember now. It was confusing me for a minute there, because you don't have an appointment time."

"What do you mean by that?" asked Brent. "I thought my appointment was today."

"Oh, it is. It's just that you don't have a time in which to be there. If you show up today, you are fine. Mr. Belcher wasn't busy today, and you were his only appointment. Now, that could all change, or course, but that's just what I was told. He just said that you can come in whenever, as long as it's before closing time, which is at 6PM." stated Mrs. Green.

"Ah," said Brent, finally realizing what Mrs. Green was trying to say. "Well, I'll leave you be, Mrs. Green, to finish up your dish washing."

"OK then, Mr. McIlrath. It was nice talking with you," Mrs. Green said, attempting to flatter Brent.

"The pleasure's all mine..." Brent then backpedaled out of the kitchen, still hearing dishes clatter from Mrs. Green's work.

"Alright, so I just need to show up today, and I'm good." Brent thought to himself, while standing in the main lobby. *"I might as well go now, that way it's done. Plus, the latest New Medicine CD came out today, so I could probably swing by the music store quick like, too. Let's see if S is here today...I'll have him drive me around."* 'S' was the nickname Brent gave to his limo driver. His real name is Samuel, but Brent just likes to call him S, for short.

Brent continued to walk forward, albeit slowly, on the slippery tile towards the living room, which was right across from the kitchen. While inching along the tiled floor, Brent added another thought to his mental "to-do list". *"God I'm hungry. Steak sounds good right about now...If I take long enough, I might be able to talk S into letting us eat at Outback Steakhouse. Even then, I'm rich, so I can do whatever the hell I want!"*

In front of him was the living room. To his immediate left, however, was a door to the faculty room. That's where Brent's workers would go and place their things (IE: purses, jackets, normal clothes, etc.) and change out into their "formal" clothing, if need be. It was a small room; it looked more like a locker room, to be honest. Unlike a locker room, however, the chance of athlete's foot in the faculty room was very small, as the faculty room was much better kept.

Finally reaching the living room, from what seemed to be an eternity of slow walking, Brent looked around to see if he could find S in there. Brent saw the couch, which faced to the right of the entryway, and towards the mounted flat screen TV on the wall; no one was lying atop the couch. The TV was turned off, so a black reflective screen is all that you could see from it. He looked to his left and saw a record player. He was curious as to if there was a record in the player, so he approached it and checked. There wasn't.

Entering the living room, Brent headed to the left, which lead to the washer and dryer, which the washer was currently running. Continuing straight through the room, Brent entered the next room; the trophy room. The trophy room, for lack there was, is mostly just a room where Brent can stroke his ego. The room contains pictures of him and his family, and, of course, trophies and awards. The only ones he earned, and weren't just consolation prizes, were a 1st place fishing trophy from when he was 17 years old, and a 2nd place trophy in the Cross-Country race for the Preston, Oklahoma charity games. These games consisted of many activities, and were held every year in May; he won the trophy this year.

Brent walked in the room and noticed an old black man wearing a long black coat was looking upon his fishing trophy. Brent walked up next to him, and the man, not turning started talking to him. "1st place Fishing Trophy in 2002, huh? That would mean that you were 17 at the time, right Brent?" The man's voice sounded much like Morgan Freeman's voice, except a little raspier.

"Yep. You got that right, S," Brent said, turning to face S.

S turned to look at Brent. S's hair was thinning and white, along with his beard; his eyes a dark shade of blue. S was adequate in muscular strength, even though he was old. S is the kind of man that could scare someone if they didn't know him all that well. Thankfully Brent does know him. "Why have you come to see me, sir?" S spoke slowly as he talked, scrunching his wrinkled forehead to show he was interested.

"I wanted to see if you could drive me into town. I know you love driving the limo…" Brent said, trying to push S into driving him.

"I do love driving the limo. What are you planning to do while in town, Brent?"

"I would like to stop by the music store and pick up a new CD," Brent said. *"Actually, I need to call up there and put a copy on hold for me. The people of this town really love to eat up the New Medicine CDs…"* Brent thought to himself, but only for a moment, as he continued to say, "I also need to stop by Mr. Belcher's place of business, about- "he was cut off by S.

"The addition to the house. Yes, yes, I know," started S. "Well, I guess I can go ahead and drive you around a little bit today. I do love driving that limo…Also; could you give me the time, please?" Brent fidgeted around in his pocket until he had a grip on his phone, he pulled it out, pressed the power button and read off the time.

"It's 11:15AM," he said. The clock changed. "Scratch that; 11:16AM."

"OK then. I guess now is a good time to go…here; you go on ahead of me. Go ahead and start up the car, will you?" S said.

"Sure thing," Brent said, as he headed to the left of the room, which had a door that lead to the garage.

"Don't forget; the keys to the limo I put in the passenger seat, underneath a jacket," added S, very quickly.

"I never have, S." Brent then opened the door to the garage, entered, and closed the door behind him.

Inside the garage, and next to the door to the right, sat the limo. There were other cars in the garage as well, almost all of them belonging to the workers. The only other car in the garage not belonging to a worker, and besides the limo, was Brent's car, which lay parked in the parking spot to the right of the limo. It was a 2006 Audi Nuvolari, which Brent liked not only because it got the job done, but because it doesn't scream, "RICH!!!" too much.

Brent walked forward towards the limo and opened the unlocked passenger seat door. He picked up the jacket lying on the seat, and grabbed the key lying underneath. He then walked around the front of the limo, and opened the driver seat and put the car into ignition. The car made a very distinct "Vrrrommmm" sound when it turned on, a sound that Brent loves to hear. He would have stayed outside of the limo, waiting for S to arrive, but it was cold in the garage, so Brent got inside the back compartment to warm himself up.

Closing the door, lights turned on inside of the limo. The front seat and passenger seat of the limo were divided from the back seat of the limo by a soundproof window that had a sliding panel; this way Brent and S could speak to each other. The only other way in which to talk to each other in the limo was to use a communication system, which was connected directly from the front seat area of the limo to the back-seat area of the limo. Brent got up from where he was sitting, and had to bend over to avoid colliding with the ceiling of the limo. He walked over to the window diving the front and back seats and opened the sliding pane. Brent then sat back down into the leather seats that the back seats provided sat there, waiting for S to arrive.

Five minutes later, the driver seat door popped open, and S sat down in the seat. "What took you so long?" Brent said, hoping to get some snarky remark from S.

"I just had to do a few things, is all. I didn't keep you waiting too long, did I, Brent?" S said back.

"Damn. That wasn't funny at all," Brent thought. He then replied, "No, not at all, S," as S was backing out the limo from the parking spot. The limo then had a little trouble getting out of the parking lot, but it was nothing that S couldn't handle. Then the limo emerged from the garage, and began driving down the path leading to the gate. Brent just stared blankly outside of the window, so fast, as the area he just jogged through sped past him in what seemed to be an instant.

A few minutes later, the limo stopped, and Brent listened in on S's and Mr. Nash's conversation. Mr. Nash spoke first, "Top 'o da mornin' to ya, Samuel!"

"And the rest of the day to you, Jon. Mind if I head on outside of the grounds?"

"Sure thing, mate," said Jon, and Brent heard a little, "Beep!" as the gate began to open. "Have fun out there! Hehehe," Jon then closed the window of his booth and Brent didn't hear him again. After a few moments of silence, the limo began to move again, made a sharp left onto the street, and off they were.

Chapter 5

-Broken Mirrors; Rise Against-

On the way into town, Brent realized he forgot to call the music store and put his CD on hold, if there is even a copy left. Brent pulled out his phone, looked up the phone number, and called the store. Thankfully, the store had a few copies left in stock, so clerk who answered the phone (Brent hopes it was a clerk!) held it behind the counter for him under the name Brent McIlrath. Brent's priority now is to get to that music store and listen to the CD.

After hanging up with the clerk, Brent hunched over and closed the pane of glass separating the front and back areas of the limo. Climbing back into his seat, Brent grabbed an auxiliary cable, which was wired into the back-compartment's speaker system, and jacked his phone to it. He turned his phone on, and brought up the music application, hit shuffle, and rocked out.

The first song that played was, "Gone Sovereign"/"Absolute Zero", by Stone Sour. "The perfect song to start with…" said Brent. As the intro to the song started, Brent began to sing along.

Brent knew almost all the words to the song. The parts he didn't know he just stayed silent for while the song continued to play. However, when the lyrics he knew came up, he sang his heart out, as if no one was watching. Singing through about half of, "Gone Sovereign", the next section of the song, titled, "Absolute Zero" started up, and Brent only knew the chorus to this song, but he preferred the second to last version of the chorus; he sang to his heart's content.

After singing the next version of the chorus, which followed the version Brent just sang, the song ended. In its place took, "Whole World's Crazy", by Art of Dying. The first verse and chorus of the song Brent sung along to.

Brent saw Art of Dying live at a no-where/no-name bar, in which New Medicine opened for. This concert took place about a year ago; last May. The concert venue wasn't very well organized, seeing as almost no one showed up to it, and the sound was horribly off. Brent didn't mind it too much, though. He still had an extravagant time, despite the horrible venue settings.

After, "Whole World's Crazy" ended, Brent decided to listen to some New Medicine, to prepare himself from the orgasmic experience was about to undergo with New Medicine's new CD. Going through all his New Medicine and A Verse Unsung songs (New Medicine's previous incarnation) he decided upon, "Resolve to Fight" from New Medicine's, "Race You to The Bottom" album. Brent, to this day, still swears that, "Race You to The Bottom is a concept album, though nothing has approved or disapproved his theory, otherwise.

Brent knew all the lyrics to this song, but he wanted to listen to the song to hear just the chorus, so he skipped around the song until he found the chorus. Whenever he finally found it, he chimed in with Jake Scherer's singing.

The song that played after, "Resolve to Fight", since the entire song list was still on shuffle, was, "Broken Mirrors", by Rise Against. "Oh, hell yes!" Brent exclaimed when he saw the name pop up on his phone, and when the opening guitar riffs started to play. "Broken Mirrors" is Brent's favorite song, so he knows every lyric. He was already a bit strained and tired of singing, since he already sang through a few songs, so he only sang his favorite part of the song, which was the last verse.

"It's been years, since our luck ran out and left us-" Brent was singing, but then stopped himself as the limo slowly came to a halt. He looked outside of the windows, and saw alleyways to his right, and a busy street, bustled with quick moving cars on both sides of the road and people walking on the sidewalks, to his left.

Brent rolled over to where his phone was laying, and, "Broken Mirrors" was still playing. Brent turned off the song, unplugged his phone, and shoved it into his right pocket. He then hunched over, and slid the glass pane open, and spoke to S. "Hey, why are we stopped? We aren't there, are we? Sure, doesn't look like it..."

S looked back at him, with concern wrote all over his face. "I don't know. The car started slowing down, and when I pressed on the gas pedal, the car didn't accelerate faster."

"Are we out of gas?"

"Not that I can tell," S said as he was looking at the gas meter, "It still has three fourths of a tank left. There must be something wrong with the motor, or something, I would assume."

"Maybe," Brent said, muffled since he had his hand over his mouth, thinking about the situation at hand. "Well, first thing's first. If something is wrong with the motor, it probably doesn't help that the car is still running. So, turn off the engine, really quick." S did as he was told. The sound of the purring motor no longer could be heard, and the sound of cars whizzing past the stalled limo were heard every so often. S also took off his seat belt, seeing as he probably won't be needing it for some time. "OK, good. S, what street are we on, do you know?"

S looked ahead, hoping to see a street sign. "Well, if my sight isn't failing me, then it seems to be that we are currently on Pringey Avenue," S said back to Brent.

"Cool. I actually know a mechanic who works down on Midway Street," Brent said, excitedly.

"Isn't Midway Street sort of...far away from here?" pondered S.

"Trust me, S. I know my way around this town pretty well. I know of a lot of shortcuts that can put me on Midway Street relatively quick."

"If you say so," S said as he sighed and sunk down into his seat.

"I got a proposition, for ya," Brent said in a southern red-neck accent, "How about I go down and talk to the mechanic that I know, and you call up a towing company to get this car towed down to the shop. That sound good?" S thought about the proposition for a few moments.

"I guess it sounds pretty solid. Besides, what other options do we really have? If you know a mechanic, then I trust that you trust him to fix our problem?"

"I trust that he will, yes."

"Well OK then, I'm sold!" S exploded, whilst slapping his hands against his thighs.

"Alright. Oh, that reminds me." Brent turned on his phone real fast and looked up "Heavy Metal, Preston, Oklahoma." on Google. "Tell the towing company to tow the car to store number 5532; the shop is called, 'Heavy Metal.'" Brent started to slide back into his seat in the back compartment, that way he could easily access the door. "Also, one more thing; make sure you stay with the limo until it gets towed. After that, you can go ahead and do whatever you like within the limits of the town. When the car gets into the shop, I'll call you-wait; you have your cell phone on you, right?"

S pulled out his cell-phone from his right jacket pocket, to show Brent that, yes, he has his cell-phone with him. It was just a normal looking flip phone, nothing fancy to it. Odd, seeing as he works for a millionaire.

"Good. I had a mild heart attack just there. Anyway, where was I...ah yes. I'll call you when the car gets into the shop, and then you can walk over to the shop and wait for the car to get done being fixed, if you'd like. I'll leave your number with the mechanic, so in case you don't want to show up early, he'll call you when he's finished working on the car. You got all that, S?"

S pretended as if he had a pen and a notepad, and was scribbling down words on the invisible notepad. "Yes sir, I think I got it all."

"You're an asshole sometimes, S. But that's why I love you so much." S grinned at his remark. "OK," Brent started, "I'm going to see the mechanic now. Take care of yourself now, S. Don't get into any trouble!"

"I can't promise that, sir," S said, still grinning like a madman.

Smirking from S's reply, Brent grasped the door handle, pulled out, and pushed out on the door, releasing natural light onto Brent. As Brent stepped out from the limo, the light blinded him from the luminous reflection of the pasty sidewalk around his area. His left arm involuntarily shifted from opening the door wider to shielding his eyes from the blinding light. As his eyes started to dilate to compensate for the sun's rays, Brent removed his arm from his eyes. He scanned the area to get familiar with his surroundings a little better. He instantly remembered the area in which he was in like the back of his hand. Brent looked in the direction that the limo was facing and saw a sign that said, "Pringey Avenue". *"Well, at least S's vision isn't failing him...yet,"* Brent thought, and smiled at his own humorous thought.

Brent, deciding to take initiative, started walking towards the mechanic's shop. In doing so, Brent had to make a 180 turn, from looking at the sign, to backtrack a bit to take the shortcuts that Brent knew about. So, he turned around and started walking.

Brent walked at his normal, brisk pace. He wasn't jogging, or fast walking, he was just walking at a normal speed, admiring and looking at the area he was around. After walking about a block or so, he saw an alleyway in between two buildings made from red brick. He turned right and entered the alleyway, since this was one of the various shortcuts in which he had to take to get to the shop quicker. He saw on the sides of the alley that there was trash littered about. On top of one of the piles was a magazine that read, "Sports Illustrated: Bikini Edition". It had, on the cover, a picture of a woman, with overly sized breasts, and she had a body that looked to be too good to be true. Brent, walking past the magazine thought to himself, *"Those issues of Sports Illustrated always seemed rather degrading towards woman. I mean, it makes them look like they're just sex symbols, and that's their only purpose. I wonder what most women think of those issues..."*

Brent, losing track of where he was going, found himself at the end of the alleyway that he was carelessly walking through. He turned left and stopped at a nearby cross-walk, which was at the end of the block. He crossed the street and then when he reached the other side of the road, turned right. In the middle of that block was another alleyway in which Brent had to turn on to get to the shop quickly. So, he turned into the alleyway and starting walking down it. Looking forward into the alleyway, he saw a man, whom looked homeless, sitting hunched over by one of the walls of the alley. *"God, I hope he's asleep. I don't want to deal with a homeless man right now..."* Brent thought to himself, as he slowly approached the hunched-over homeless man. As he approached, Brent tried not to make eye contact, let alone look at the man, in hopes that he could avoid anything that would slow him down. Despite his best efforts, he got "caught".

In a gruff and quiet voice, the man looked up and said, "Do you have any change that you can spare, good man?"

"Shit!" Brent thought, as his face winced. He still wasn't looking at the man. *"Well, I do have those dollars that I put into my jacket earlier. I guess I'll be a nice guy and give the man a dollar, or two."* He started to think a little more, and started to kind of feel bad for the homeless man. Brent has everything; he's rich, healthy, people who work under him. What did this poor man have? Nothing.

Brent, now with a little more enthusiasm, turned to face the homeless man and said, while turning, "I have a dollar or two I can spare, yes." He dug out two dollars from his jacket pocket, and looked up to give the man the money.

"Here you are-" Brent's jaw dropped, as did the homeless man's. Brent's money dropped from his hand and onto the cold and semi-damp concrete. That was the only noise either of the two men heard, as both of their senses, and worlds, stopped.

Chapter 6

-Before Tomorrow Comes; Alterbridge-

Brent looked upon the homeless man with elongated complexity, as did the homeless man towards Brent. After a while of silence and staring, Brent finally spoke the first word.

"P-…P-Patrick?" Brent let out, very confused, and very soft.

Patrick looked just like any other homeless man that you would see walking down the street. He was very thin, although he wasn't entirely "skin-and-bones". Patrick looked to be a muscular man; someone who would beat you down if you got into a fight with him. He wore an army green colored hooded jacket, which covered up a green undershirt, which had little tears at the bottom lining of the shirt. Below the waist, he wore run-of-the-mill jeans, with a few holes in various places; his shoes were just normal looking green colored shoes, with a few mud stains here and there. Upon the facial region lay a light-brown beard, though it looked to be sort of controlled, and no mustache to speak of. His head was covered by an army green beanie hat, which covered most of his long brown hair; some of his hair peeped out, though. His eyes, along with most of his attire, were also a shade of green.

"Brent?" Patrick's voice was still very gruff sounding and sharp. So much so, that it hurt Brent's throat just hearing him speak. "Brent McIlrath?"

"Patrick! It is you!" Brent exclaimed.

"Yup; Patrick Armstrong. Don't wear it out. You never answered my question, though. You are Brent McIlrath, right?"

"24 hours a day, seven days a week," Brent replied, with a smile that you would see a child have after receiving the gift they've been asking for on Christmas.

"Well I be damned-wait, hold on a second." Patrick then started to cough vigorously, and overtime spat out a clump of mucus from his mouth. "Whew," Patrick said afterwards. His voice was much smoother sounding now. "Sorry about that, Brent. I have to make my voice sound like that, or else no one believes I'm a homeless guy. I have to buy into the "stereotype" that people always think of when they picture, 'homeless'."

Brent paid no mind to what Patrick was saying about having to fake his voice, as he was still flabbergasted to see Patrick standing there.

"Patrick!"

"Yeah, hi, Brent. I didn't notice you standing there."

"Oh my God, how long has it been?" said Brent, finally starting to form sentences again, and neglecting the previous comment made by Patrick.

"Actually, I was about to ask you the same thing." Patrick started to stand up, and eventually stood on two feet and peered at Brent, face to face. Patrick was a few inches taller than Brent, as Brent was 5'10", and Patrick was 6'0". "How long has it been?" Patrick put his hand up into his beanie and started scratching his head.

"I think it's been, what, 7 years, was it?" Brent said, coming up with an answer.

"Yeah that sounds about right. Yeah, that should be it," Patrick leaned back onto the wall that he was close to, "because I remember we tried to use fake I.D.s to get into that one bar...I don't remember the name of it..."

"The Chorus," Brent said, helping Patrick. Brent was kind of taken off guard by his own response. He had totally forgotten about that night, and he just suddenly remembered the name of the bar? Brent didn't really pay much mind to this, though.

"The Chorus, yes, thank you," Patrick said, breaking Brent's confusion and thought. "We tried to use fake I.D.s when we were 20 to get into The Chorus, and we got caught! Oh, that was a scary moment, I remember." Patrick said, with a glisten in his eyes.

"That was scary, yes." Brent said, with his hand clinching the back of his neck. "So, how've you been doing in the past 7 years? What's been up with you?" Brent asked.

"Well, if you haven't figured it out already, things have not been 'up' recently. I think it's pretty clear that I'm, well, homeless," Patrick moved his hands from his upper torso to his thighs. "So, I'm going to leave my answer with: Not so good. But what of you, Mr. "I'm wearing a fancy suit and tie"; how've you been? What's been 'up' with you?"

"Well," Brent started, "things have been going pretty OK with me, being rich and all..."

"Wait, hold up. You're rich? I don't remember that! When did that happen?" Patrick was very confused, and his veins popped out from his head as he tried to remember.

"...Yeah...I've always been rich. I was born into a wealthy family, don't you remember?"

"Not really...I don't remember you ever being even remotely rich. I remember that you and your family were middle-class, at best; as was I. You always had a little more money than my family, yes, but I don't say that would classify you as, 'rich'."

Brent stared awkwardly at Patrick, thinking that he might be delusional, being homeless and all.

"Anyway..." Brent continued, "besides that, I'm doing fine. Nothing to say, really." Brent suddenly remembered that he had to go see the mechanic about his limo. "Ohhh, oh crap! Arg!"

"What? Huh? What's happening?" Patrick exclaimed, as he looked down the alleyway that they were in.

"It's nothing concerning you, so don't worry. The reason I was walking down this alleyway in the first place was so that I could take a shortcut to a mechanic's shop. You see, my limo broke down-" he was cut off.

"YOU HAVE A LIMO, TOO?" Patrick yelled; his day just kept getting better and better.

Disregarding Patrick's comment, Brent went on.

"...on Pringey Avenue, and the shop is on Midway Street. So, I better start going again, it was nice seeing y-..., would you like to go to the mechanic's shop with me? We could continue to catch up that way."

"Yeah, sure. I mean, it's not like I have anything else better to do anyways." Patrick was on board with this idea full-heartedly.

"OK then, let's get moving!"

Patrick stepped away from the wall that he was leaning on. As Brent started to walk forward, and down the rest of the alley, Patrick slinked back and picked up those two dollars that Brent dropped earlier. He stuffed them into one of his jacket pockets and sprinted up next to Brent, and then began to keep up with Brent's speed.

Reaching the end of the alley, Brent started to go left; Patrick stopped him.

"Where the hell are you going?"

"I'm taking the shortcut to the mechanic's shop," Brent said, a little confused by Patrick's intake to the situation.

"Nonononono, we're going right. Trust me; I know this town better than you think you do. So, follow me; I'll get us to that shop faster than your shortcut will."

Ultimately, Brent decided to trust Patrick in leading him to the shop.

"Just so you know, the shop is called, "Heavy Metal". Store number 5532." Brent said, after they have been walking for a little while.

"You just memorized that earlier today, didn't you?" Patrick said, as he looked back over his shoulder at Brent, who was walking just slightly behind him.

"No...yes...shut up."

Patrick chuckled. Brent caught up with Patrick as they were walking down a sidewalk, passing up multiple shops along the way. Most of them were bakeries.

Brent began the war of questions, "How is your family doing, Patrick? Or do you not really know?"

"Well...they're OK, I guess. Still kind of idiots; douchebags, too. I'm homeless due to them. We all got in a big fight, so I moved out and decided that living on the streets would be better than living with them. It's a very short story, but it's short and to the point."

"I'm sorry to hear that." Brent said, sounding very sincere.

"Nah, it's fine. Not your fault anyway. Although, I do have a question for you." Brent's ears perked up at the sound of Patrick's question. "How is it that you got rich?"

"I never remember you asking me that when we were younger..." started Brent.

"Yeah, because you were never rich..." Patrick said under his breath. Brent didn't hear him, and continued with what he was saying.

"I can't say why, legally, but I can tell you that my father made some pretty good investments a while back, and the money train just hasn't stopped rolling." Brent had a good laugh at that, but Patrick just kept walking forward, unaffected.

"So...what's it like being homeless?" Brent asked, very subtly.

"Yeah, I was waiting for you to ask that, Brent." Patrick said back, as if he already expected the topic to come up.

"Sorry."

"No, it's perfectly OK. In fact, I want to ask you what it's like to be rich, but I think I already know the answer to that one." Brent chuckled a little. "So, to answer your question; bottom line: It's not all that bad, to be honest. I mean, yeah having money is nice and all, but being homeless has made me realize a lot of things. Like how much I like to run."

"No way, I love to run too," Brent added.

Patrick seemed to ignore this comment, as he continued, "Actually, being homeless has also shown me how beautiful nature can be. Ironic, seeing as my "home", for lack it is, lies between a dark alleyway with little light entering it, but that's beside the point. Being hungry, cold, and ignored all the time, though, that sucks..." Patrick paused and tried to concentrate on what he really wanted to know. "Back to you, though. Are you still as big of a music freak as you were back in High School? Do you listen to music as much as you used to?"

"...why did you ask?" Brent turned the question around on Patrick.

"...because I still am...and I still do..." Patrick replied, seeming very retained. He peered past Brent and looked both ways of the street that they were at. The path was clear, as Brent and Patrick trekked across the crosswalk.

"Oh, make no mistake, my good friend, I think I'm an even bigger music freak than I was in High School!" Brent said, smiling.

"I honestly don't think that's possible," Patrick jokingly said.

", I want to ask; how are you still a music nerd, seeing as you're...well..." Brent tried to think of a better word to use in place of, "homeless."

"...homeless?" Patrick finished Brent's sentence. Brent just nodded. Patrick then continued, "Yeah, well, it's not very easy," Patrick started to say, "You see, I make a little bit of money by begging for it every day, and by searching through trash and such. It's not very often, but overtime, when I save up enough cash, and after purchasing a few necessities that help make doing daily tasks easier, I go to the music store and buy myself an album. Like I said, it isn't very often that this happens, but it does happen on occasion."

"OK then, next question," Brent started to say, "even if you do buy the album, you can't listen to it. Do you just have a jukebox that you carry around on your shoulder all the time?"

"I know you were joking, but kind of, yes," Patrick looked past Brent again and looked both ways before they crossed another crosswalk. "I found a working radio one day going through a trash can, and it played CDs still. So, I've been using that to listen to my music, whether it is via CD or just local radio."

Brent, still a little confused by this, kept pressing Patrick on the subject. "And no one has tried to steal your radio or your 'extensive CD collection'?"

"Surprisingly, no. I keep my radio and CDs hidden underneath the dumpster that was in the alley where we met up earlier. I keep them cloaked underneath my blanket and pillow that I sleep on at night. So far no one's seen it, or taken it I should say, so I guess my hiding place works."

Brent and Patrick stopped at the stoplight that was ahead of them, and waited for the walk signal to turn on. After a few seconds, it turned, and Brent and Patrick crossed the street. "Turn left here," Patrick said, and Brent followed instruction and turned left. They were now walking along the side of a park. Children could be heard playing on the playground; Brent looked over and saw a swing set, with two little kids, no older than five, swinging on them. There was also a red colored slide, which was littered with little children taking turns sliding down the slide. Benches were a fair distance away from all the equipment, on which the parents were sitting, watching their children play, ready to spring to the rescue if anything were to go wrong. The only thing dividing Brent and Patrick from the organized chaos was the chain-link fence that Brent was walking along side. Brent felt a sudden sense of deja-vu, for some reason...he couldn't quite figure out why.

"Jumping back to an earlier topic," Brent started to say, "you said you liked to run, correct?"

Patrick looked at Brent, instead of at the sidewalk in front of them. "Yeah. What of it?"

"Well, I said that I also liked to run. I figured I could use that to sort-of bleed into what it's like to live, 'the good life'."

Patrick thought of the offer. "OK, I had my turn in the limelight, why not you? So yeah, tell me of a day in the life of Brent McIlrath."

Brent chuckled a little at the thought. "OK, well I wake up every day and I run about four miles, since the distance from my..." Brent, who was grinning from ear to ear, since he really wanted to hear Patrick's reaction to how his day went, looked at Patrick. "...mansion..."

"OK, please. Just stop." Brent burst out into laughter. Patrick went on, "Stop right now before I drown you in my tears of sorrow." Patrick was very straightforward when saying this. It made Brent laugh even more.

"Anyway," Brent started to say, through elongated laughs here and there, "the distance from my mansion to the gate, which lies in front of a windy road, is about two miles. I just run down to the gate, turn around, and come back, so it ends up being about 4 miles in total; give or take a few feet."

"I swear, since I'm still trying to wrap my head around the idea, that I don't remember you being rich when we were friends in Middle School and High School," Patrick continued to press Brent on this subject.

"Well maybe you're going crazy, since I'm pretty sure that I've been rich all my life, and I would know." Brent said this, not trying to be rude, or harsh, but in a joking sense.

"Yeah, well I'm not budging from my thought...regardless, mind explaining to me what all goes on in your mansion; such as the rooms, how expansive is the house, do you have people that work for you?" Patrick's voice got really excited at the last thing he wanted to ask Brent about the mansion.

"Well, if you want to, when the limo gets fixed and I head back home, I could take you back with me. You could spend the night; get a good night's sleep for once. New clothes, a nice shower..."

"Really?" Patrick quickly changed his mood. "I mean- uh...nah, I don't want to be a burden."

"Burden? Please, it would be my treat if you could come to the house. We haven't seen each other in so long! Plus, it's hard to explain, but it just feels...right to me, you know? Like it's supposed to be done."

From that line, Brent and Patrick stayed silent for about a minute or so; during this time, they crossed another crosswalk, and turned left at the end of that block. Brent brought up the next topic.

"Hey, mind if I say something?"

"Why the hell do you think I would care?" Patrick said, very quickly.

"Well, OK then. I don't mean to sound rude or something like that, and maybe it's just me, but I never thought about you until we met today. Did you do the same thing to me?"

Patrick sighed. "To be honest, yeah I did the same thing. In fact, I totally forgot you existed until just a little bit ago. That makes me sound like a bad person, I know, but it's true. Which is odd, because I remember us being, like, the best of friends; inseparable, even!"

"No, you're not a bad person for forgetting," Brent followed up, "I forgot too! Wow, I sound like a dick." Patrick laughed. "And yeah, I remember us being the best of friends, as well. Do you remember why we even stopped being friends? Because I'm drawing a blank."

"No, I can't think of it either. Huh. Weird." Patrick eyes looked at the clear blue sky that was above him.

Brent and Patrick, while lost in thought, walked past their old High School. "Preston High School" it read in bold black letters on the front of the school. An analog clock sat below the lettering; it read 12:24PM. Brent looked over at the High School, and his eyes were drawn to the clock. When he read the time, he remembered how hungry he was. His stomach gurgled. *"Have to get the limo fixed first, then food,"* He told himself. While he was beating this idea into his head, Patrick began to speak.

"Hey, Brent, remember all of our old friends when we were in High School?"

"Hmm? Oh, yeah! I wonder how most of them are doing..."

"Yeah. Who were all of them again? I remember Chris and Polly, Jenna...Kevin...Remi..." Patrick was starting to count the names on his fingers. *"Huh...weird...I forgot those people existed until just right now...just how like I was with Brent's existence..."* Patrick thought to himself. He passed It off as he's just a bad person, and moved on.

Brent chimed in, "Ken, Jaime, Nick, Emily and Evan, if I am remembering correctly." Patrick nodded in agreement. "Actually, I'm been in touch with two of them; Ken and Jaime."

"Really?" Patrick asked, "Tell me more, tell me more!" He was trying to quote *Grease*, but it didn't turn out as well as he hoped. His reaction was rather odd, because Patrick always secretly hated Ken, unbeknownst to Brent. Ken was always a bit of a douche, at least to Patrick, but Patrick put up with him, because Brent and Ken were pretty good friends, and Patrick figured it was the nice thing to do. Jaime, on the other hand, he loved. He was always kind and generous to

Patrick and Brent, always helping them out on things. Patrick always felt as if Jaime was hanging out with the wrong group of people, though.

"Ken is actually the owner of the mechanic shop that we are heading to, 'Heavy Metal'. Jaime is now the owner of his own architecture company, which is where I was going to go to, but then my limo broke down. Well, after I stopped by the music store, to get the latest New Medicine CD. You see, I was going to get an addition onto my mansion-I should stop while I'm ahead, right?"

"Yeah," Patrick said, not being able to keep a straight face. "But what was that you said about a New Medicine CD? Is there one?"

"Uh-huh. I have it on hold at the music shop, that way I don't have to worry about not being able to get it. With the way today's turning out, I might not be able to actually get it until tomorrow."

"Oh man! Dude, I've gotta get that eventually, when the money's right of course. I loved 'Race You to The Bottom'! Patrick was getting hyper over the whole, "New Medicine" topic. "It killed me on the inside when they were played here last May and I couldn't afford to go. Granted, I used that money to provide me certain things for a few more days, but I so wanted to see them."

", not to toot my own horn or anything, but I was actually at that show."

"You're kidding," Patrick said, flabbergasted.

"You keep forgetting that I'm rich," Brent said light heartedly.

"It's pretty easy seeing as you weren't rich…I swear he wasn't…right?" Patrick kept this thought to himself, and instead said, "Yeah, I guess I do, huh?"

", in the past few years, I've been to a bunch of concerts. I was at a Green Day concert, a Tenacious D concert, the Rockstar Uproar Festival 2011 and 2012, Vans Warped Tour 2012, the New Medicine show, in which they opened for Art of Dying, Coheed and Cambria, Hoobastank, and Foo Fighters, in which Rise Against opened for them."

Patrick's jaw was unhinged so far that saying it dropped would be an understatement. "Wow...I mean, wow...I've only been to two concerts in my entire life. And I was with you both times. It was the Aerosmith concert we went to when we were in 8th grade, and that Fall Out Boy concert that we went to when we were juniors in High School."

The two continued to walk down the sidewalk. From this point on it was just a straight path to Ken's shop. After a few seconds of silence, Patrick made a hand motion, as if he was pulling on the horn of a train, and made the sounds, "Toot toot." They both had a good laugh at that.

"So, Patrick," Brent said, after it was silent for a few short moments, "what CDs do you have back at your...is it effective to call it, 'home'?"

"I guess so, yeah. It's probably the best way to describe it."

"Yeah, OK then. What CDs do you have at your home?" Brent asked.

Patrick didn't hold back with his answer.

"I own the albums, "American Idiot", "21st Century Breakdown", "Race You to The Bottom", "Infinity on High", "Endgame", "Appeal to Reason", and my newest addition, "House of Gold & Bones Part 1.""

"You have the new Stone Sour album?"

"Yep, I just got it a few days ago. It kicks a lot of ass, I must say."

"Oh yeah it does," Brent said.

A few seconds after this conversation ended, the two reached the mechanic's shop. "Well, here we are," Patrick said, sounding a little proud.

"That really was quicker than my way. Probably a lot safer; cleaner, too."

"Well, I try."

And with that pompous remark, Brent opened the door to the shop, and the two walked inside holding their heads up high, having no clue what would be in store for them in the coming hour.

Chapter 7

-One; Metallica-

As the duo slowly walked into the shop, they were greeted with a few chairs to their right and a potted plant on their left. In front of them was a secretary sitting diligently behind her desk; her eyes were in a trance from the computer she stared at. She turned her attention from the computer when she heard the chime that a bell, which was hung onto the door, made from Brent and Patrick's entry. She said to them:

"Hello! What can I help you with?"

Brent advanced towards the secretary as Patrick stood back, looking at the contents that the room held. It was very barren; the only things in the room were the white walls, blue carpeting, the chairs, the plant, the secretary desk, and desktop computer that sat behind the secretary desk, which was more than likely for work related things. There was also a door that was embedded into the right of the desk. The room was rather depressing.

Brent approached the secretary desk.

"Hello..." he looked at the name pin that was attached to her jacket, which overlaid a plain white shirt, and had a "V" cut on the collar of the shirt. The name pin read, "Secretary: Heavy Metal – Pam".

"...Pam," continued Brent. Pam smiled and straightened up in her seat. The fact that Brent looked at her pin to search for her name amused her, strangely. "I'm here to see Ken Sinclair. My car broke down and I wanted to see if he could repair it. That is, when the tow truck brings it down to the shop." Pam turned around in her chair and started typing into her computer.

"OK, Mr. Sinclair is in back working on a car right now, so you might have to wait a couple of minutes until he's finished," Pam said, still typing into the computer. Brent watched to lean over the desk to see what she was doing, but he fought off the temptation.

"Actually, I wanted to see if I could speak with Mr. Sinclair on a personal level. I've been his friend since High School, and I wanted to talk to him a bit before my car came in. Could that be arranged?" Brent asked, with puppy dog eyes.

"Well..." Pam scratched the knuckles of her right hand with the fingers of the left. She studied Brent, looking at his clothing. She noticed the suit he was wearing looked moderately dirty. Her face scrunched in doubt, but she didn't feel like asking Brent about it. Instead she said, in an almost irritated tone, "I guess you can go back. He should be almost done, anyway."

"Thank you, Pam!" Brent then motioned to Patrick, whom entered the door to Ken alongside Brent. As Patrick started to walk through the door with Brent, Pam stopped him.

"Umm...where do you think you're going, sir?"

Brent helped Patrick out of this one.

"Don't' worry, ma'am; he's with me."

Pam looked at Patrick, seeing all his disgusting features on his clothes. Mud and dirt, water stains; the works.

"OK, I guess you can go in, too. Just don't distract Mr. Sinclair too much, please?"

"We won't," said Brent as he walked through the doorway and into the garage; Patrick followed right behind him, moping.

The garage was a frigid ice box. The floors were made of cement, as were the walls; the room was boxed in, with the only exists being the exit door located on the far end of the room and the multiple garage doors, which were closed at the current moment. The ceiling was just steel girders, which held up an aluminum-like material, acting as the roof. The ceiling also had air vents, which could help release any toxic fumes that could accumulate inside of the workshop. The only source of any heat would be from a heater, which was being propped up against the wall, not plugged into any electrical outlet. Oddly, though, sound didn't seem to create an echo whilst Brent and Patrick walked across the floor.

"Brrr, Jesus Christ, it's cold in here," Brent said, as he slid his hands up and down his arms, trying to create warmth through friction.

"Eh, I've been through worse," Patrick said as he looked at his multiple layers of clothing that he was wearing. Secretly though, he was a little cold in this room. But he wasn't going to let Brent know that.

The two continued to exit the doorway, making sure to close the door behind them, and out into the center of the room. In the distance, they saw a car, with a man underneath it. He was sitting on a creeper, and moving his hands all around the underbelly of the car. A radio sat next to him and as he worked, as well as a stool, which sat to one side of the car.

As the two approached the car and the man, the sound coming from the radio could be distinctly heard. Both Brent and Patrick registered that the radio was playing the song, "Madhouse", by Anthrax. As the two got closer to the busy man, Brent started the conversation:

"Excuse me sir, sorry to bother you, but we wanted to know where we could find a Mr. Ken Sinclair? The fourth?" Brent added.

The man put his hands down from the underside of the car, and rolled out, with his back on the creeper. He put down the tools he was using, and sat up on his creeper, and answered Brent's question.

"Ken Sinclair the fourth; that is I. Who's askin'-Is that you, Brent?" His eyes looked upon Brent's face, studying it to see if his postulate was correct.

"Yessir, it is."

"Oh my God...it's been so long since I saw you last!" Ken seemed flabbergasted and amazed to see Brent standing there right before his very eyes.

"Yeah, I know," Brent replied. "How are you doing?" he asked.

"Ah, I've been great, thanks for asking! How've you been?" Ken asked. He sat more upright on his creeper. He leaned over to turn off the radio. His face held a 5 O'clock shadow, and freckles all throughout his cheeks. His head had very minuscule amounts of hair on it; thinning would be a good word to describe it. Ken was wearing a t-shirt that had the name of a recent car show on it; faded, though. It had a picture of a 1970 Plymouth Superbird beneath the letting of the car show's name. It was unreadable, thanks to the font style. The grease, oil, and food stains on the shirt also didn't help, either. He also wore torn up jeans, with some of the holes patched together. Overall, Ken was a very manly man, and average size, too; not too big, but not too small either. He also breathed very heavily for some reason. ", don't answer that quite yet," Ken started to say, "Who's that with ya there, poor ol' Brent?"

"Really? I thought you might have recognized him, considering we all used to be friends in High School," Brent said with a skeptical look on his face. "Ken, allow me to reintroduce you to Patrick." Ken's eyes widened and squinted, trying to remember who this, "Patrick" character was. "...Armstrong," Brent said, very blankly.

"......You're shitting me, right?" Ken's expression changed from confused to a sort of sarcastic/doubtful look. He started to laugh at the thought of seeing Patrick again. Brent joined in on the laughter, chuckling a bit. Patrick just stood there; impassive. "Yeah, now that you mention it," Ken added, "I see a little bit of Patrick physique to him! Hehe, sorry 'bout being sort of cold to ya, just haven't seen you in so long, you know? And you look so different; in a good way..." Ken said that last part without much feeling or emotion to it.

"Yeah, I know...and don't worry; this room is cold enough to suffice," Patrick said back to Ken.

"Eh, well it's not so cold to me, seeing as I'm workin' on these cars almost all-day long. Funny, since I'm a mechanical engineer and this is just a side-job I do. Mostly because I like it, but the extra payroll doesn't hurt, either." Ken took a quick look around the room. "I'm actually the only person that works at this shop. I don't have any other workers, except for Ms. Pam in the lobby." He broke his speech, and said very quietly, "I've actually got my eye on that pretty little lady. I've been thinking of asking her out on a date for a while now. Just haven't brought up the courage to do it yet…"

"Really?" started Brent, "You must be just rolling in the dough, huh? And, hey, best of luck with the lady situation! I hope it all works out!" Brent never really thought anything of the secretary; , he thought that she was kind of a bitch, but he didn't want to say that to Ken's face.

"Thanks." He chuckled and blushed, both at once. "So, how have your love lives been going? Find any girls yet, you two?"

"No, not yet," Brent said. He looked over at Patrick, "I forgot to ask earlier, any female that you're interested in, old pal?"

"No, but thanks for reminding me," Patrick said, being sarcastic.

"So," Brent started, after a few moments of silence, plus he wanted to keep the conversation moving, "what kind of car are you working on there, Ken?"

"Well, it's a 2002 Ford Taurus. Why you wondering, Brent?"

"Oh, no reason. Just trying to make friendly conversation, I guess. So why are you working on it; what's wrong with it?"

"I could tell you," Ken said, "but I would just end up going off, saying jargon that neither of you would understand. So, I won't say anything other than that it's something that I need to work under the car for."

"Well we're sorry if we interrupted you, Ken. Do you want us to go wait out in the lobby for a little bit…?" Patrick said, hoping to escape from Ken.

"Nah, its fine. I was almost done anyway. Just give me, like, 30 more seconds and we can talk then, k?" He laid back down on his creeper, and grabbed a tool and started moving his hands again.

"Sure thing, take your time." Brent was hoping it wouldn't take more than 30 seconds.

"If you two want," Ken's voice was muffled from the car, "you can grab some foldable chairs; we have a few on the wall to my left." Brent and Patrick looked to their right, and saw a few foldable chairs lying against the wall. They walked over, and carried them back to where they were a few moments ago. They unfolded the chairs, and sat down in them. Not but seconds after Brent and Patrick sat back down, Ken emerged from under the car, with a new stain on his already stained shirt. He got up from his creeper, pushed it aside, and grabbed a nearby towel in which to wipe off his sweaty face. He pulled up the stool that was near the car and sat down on it, and asked Brent and Patrick a question.

"Hey, I was thinking of something when I was down under the car. Remember when we used to call Patrick, 'Dirty Harry' because his hair was always really long and dirty?"

"Sadly, yes..." Patrick said, in a very chastened tone. *"Harry...Harry...? That reminds me of something, but I don't exactly of what, though..."* Patrick thought to himself.

Ken started to laugh a bit. Brent, suddenly remembering, started to laugh as well, just remembering the dumb nickname they gave Patrick.

Ken then recollected another fond memory of the younger days, "You two remember that one time, in 7th grade, when we poured paint thinner on Mrs. Phipps' math tests?"

Patrick spoke up and said, "Yeah, I remember that. Oh yeah, because we all thought that we did horrible on that test, so we poured paint thinner on her papers during lunch!"

Brent jumped in on the reminiscing.

"Hey, you guys remember when we were in 8th grade and we spray painted all the walls? We just put random designs on the walls, too!"

"Yeah, and I remember that the teachers were trying to find out who it was, and one of our designs looked like a J and a W, so they punished Jake Walsh for it!" Ken started laughing hysterically. Brent laughed too, but not as bad. Patrick just chuckled at the thought. After they had their good laugh, Brent started to laugh again, thinking of another moment.

"Hey, hey. Remember," He couldn't stop laughing, "remember when we were freshmen in High School and Patrick got into that huge fight with, who was it...?" He looked towards Patrick for an answer. Patrick just looked down at the floor, as if regretting that decision above all the other stupid stunts he did as a young tot.

Ken, though, stepped in and "helped' Patrick out.

"Yeah, I know who you're talking about. I think his name was Steve Blunt." Ken started chuckling, seeing as he knew what came next in the story and he was just dying to hear it be told again.

Brent continued, "Yeah, so Patrick and Steve got into this huge fight because Steve kept being a douche to you, so you turned around and punched him in the gut," Brent and Ken started cracking up, "and then we jumped in to help you, then Steve's friends joined in," Brent broke the story for a minute so he could get a few laughs out of his system. Brent continued, though broken laughs, "and then, like, four or five other people joined into the fight for no reason!" Brent and Ken started laughing so hard that they were crying. Patrick was still staring at the floor, trying to think of something else to occupy his brain. He went back to his previous thought of, "Harry". *"Why does that name remind me of something…ugh, I don't know. This is going to kill me…"* He continued to think as the other two laughed like drunken hyenas.

"But the best part," Brent was gasping for air at this point, "was that none of us got caught! It was just Steve and his friends, and the people that joined in randomly!" The two-kept laughing and crying and gasping for air. Patrick still sat there, unaffected.

"Yeah, I remember that! Hahaha, we were little ol' assholes in our time, weren't we?" Ken said, half laughing through the sentence. He wiped away tears that were running down from his face.

"Yeah…yeah…" said Patrick. He was still looking down at the floor, still thinking, but coming up short. He now started to twiddle his thumbs. He could hear the laughs of Ken and Brent still, and he could almost tell that they were crying; he didn't even have to look up.

"Oh, lighten up, would ya, Henry?" Ken said, jokingly. Although, after releasing the sentence from his lips, Ken's eyes widened, his face grew pale, and his lips clenched, as well as his hands. His back became straight as an arrow. His deep breathing, which had been apparent to Brent and Patrick before, became much more noticeable.

Suddenly, something clicked in Patrick's mind. Fragments of memories began rushing back to him. Thoughts of times where he hung out at people's houses, and hanging out with friends all started to form themselves together. He started to recall conversations, all with everyone referring to him as "Henry". Patrick even recalled writing down the name "Henry" on papers in school.

Patrick's head started to swell thinking about all of this, and remembering things he hadn't known he ever knew before. Brent was feeling a mutual type of recollection; Brent recalled both his and Patrick's parents referring to Patrick as "Henry". Brent even started to remember referring to Patrick as "Henry" in some of his memories, too. While his head hurt with the sudden impact of memories as well, he was more concerned for himself. If he suddenly remembered the name "Henry" and it made such an impact on his memories, what of him? A cold chill was sent down Brent's spine. He shivered. Patrick also felt this cold chill.

Plus, it didn't add up to them; why does this name of Henry suddenly mean so much to these two? Brent and Patrick surely must have heard the name "Henry" before this moment, but for some reason now it means much more.

"I'm sorry, what did you just call me, Ken?" Patrick asked, in a very nervous, yet bellicose tone.

"What? Huh? Oh…umm…nothing…Patrick," Ken shuttered. His palms were starting to sweat.

"No, I heard that too," Brent interrupted, "Why did you just call Patrick, 'Henry'?"

Ken's eyes shifted all around, but mostly his pupils sat in the upper-left corner of his eye sockets. After a little while, it looked like he shut himself down like a computer, for he slinked over and held his head down low. Almost as if he was hoping the whole situation would just blow over.

Brent and Patrick leaned in real close to each other and began whispering a battle-plan.

Brent began: "Please tell me I'm not the only thinking this is a little weird."

Patrick: "Trust me, I'm more than convinced that something's up."

"Yeah...I don't know why, but I'm recalling past events that I never have before...and the name 'Henry' is in all of them. You're the one being referred to as 'Henry' in my memories."

"I'm the same way." Patrick's hands began to shake wildly, and his fingers clenched themselves into a fist. His legs also looked like he could spring up from the chair at any moment. "How should we deal with this? I feel like there's something more to this thing than just a feeling of doubt I have."

"I feel the same," Brent whispered, sounding almost sad. "It could just be something dumb, but I feel there's more behind it than that. And Ken," the two looked over at him. He still looked dead. "Ken might be our only way of finding out."

"Yeah..." Patrick's whole body began to shake now, his fists becoming more and more compressed as time went on. "I say we go over there and beat the shit out of him." He gritted his teeth and said, "If he values his life, he'll give us some information before I kill him."

Brent became very defensive, "No, no. Let's leave that for a last resort..." Brent never really did enjoy fighting, or violence at all for that matter. He especially hated it when he knew he could do nothing to stop or prevent it; he always wanted to do his best to leave fighting for the last option. Brent continued, "I'll try to talk to him and see if he'll give up easily. Who knows? That might be all we have to do to get him to talk."

"And if he doesn't comply easily?" Patrick asked, almost in complete hatred.

Brent sighed, and then said, "Then you can go in and be more assertive." Patrick smiled, and the two then turned to both face Ken once more.

"Ken," Brent began. Ken was still trying to duck out of any conflict. Brent decided to just press on with what he was saying, "Ken, you aren't going to get very far by sitting there ignoring us, hoping we'll just forget about what just happened. I'm starting to recall things, Patrick as well, all with the name

'Henry' in them. It's driving me crazy not knowing why this name means so much suddenly. I'm obsessing over it." He said that last bit sounding as if he was going to burst into tears at any moment. Ken looked up for the first time during all of this. He made eye contact with Brent as he went on, "Now we could sit here all day and feed into excuses, and fabricated imaginations that you would keep making to save your own skin, but it would just be easier if you tell us the truth. It's obvious that you're hiding something from us, and we," Brent made a hand motion to show that he was talking about himself and Patrick, "are hell-bent on finding out why 'Henry' means something to both of us. We share a common feeling; not sure what that feeling is, but it's something that makes us sure there's something more to this. So just give it up, Ken; tell us now. We're your friends here."

Ken broke his eye contact with Brent and stared at the floor once more. He did this for almost a full minute. His fingers were locked together, clenching in and out. Ken stayed silent; he wasn't going to back down just because Brent asked nicely.

After a little while, Brent looked over to Patrick (who looked ready to go into war), and said, in a defeated tone, "Go for it."

Patrick smiled and began to laugh as he stood up from his chair. He walked over to Ken and punched him as hard as he could in the cheek. Ken seemed dazed from this, and was knocked off his chair and onto the cold, hard floor. He looked up at Patrick, paralyzed, with shock and fear in his eyes. Patrick turned around and found a discarded wrench near the car that Ken was working on. He picked it up and walked back over to Ken. He grabbed him by the scruff of his shirt and hoisted him back onto his feet. He pushed him backwards onto the hood of the car. Patrick grabbed the wrench with both hands, and swung downward onto Ken's left shoulder. Ken let out a scream of pain while Patrick did the same procedure on his other shoulder. Ken's scream became much more blood-curling, and Brent's shoulders began to hurt just by watching.

While Ken was trying to get over the pain, Patrick leaned in real close and said, with the wrench held close to Ken's head, "Now tell us what you know, or this wrench and I will be the headline of tomorrow's paper." Ken still said nothing; the only thing that came out of his mouth was deep breaths and the occasional gasp of pain. "Well, it's your body..." Patrick said, as he swung the wrench like a baseball bat towards Ken's jaw. The impact was so loud and damaging that it sent a ring all throughout the workshop. Brent's body winced at the sound, and Ken's body was flung to the floor with a hard collapse. Brent stood up and yelled, "Patrick, stop!"

"Sit back down, Brent," Patrick said back, in an almost demented voice. "I have this under control..." Patrick began to advance towards Ken, and readied himself to make yet another blow upon his body.

As he raised the wrench in the air, Ken yelled, from the floor, "Stop!" Patrick stopped, and Ken turned his head to the side so that Patrick could hear him better. Ken's face looked bloodied, and shattered. He opened his mouth and spit out blood; it flowed out like a small river. Ken said, sounding gargled, "I'll talk..." He collapsed onto the floor completely. Patrick motioned for Brent to come over and help, then the two picked up Ken off the floor and positioned him on his chair; he was almost limp. Brent and Patrick sat down in their respective spots, Patrick still with the wrench positioned comfortably in his right hand. Ken started to move a bit more now, and opened his mouth; blood poured out. He spat it out onto the floor, and Brent noticed that Ken's mouth had a few teeth misaligned, and his jaw was nowhere near where it should be. All this aside, Ken spoke, albeit quietly, "I called him Henry..." he spat blood once more. He grunted, and finished his sentence, "...because that's his real name."

"What?!" Brent and Patrick both exclaimed at the same time. They looked at one another and exchanged expressions that the other had.

"It's true," Ken said, sounding a little more mushed-mouth. Regardless, he continued to talk: "And you aren't left out of this either, Brent."

"Me too?" Brent was becoming more confused now. "Tell us, Ken. Tell us more!" Brent was agitated now.

"OK. I want both of you to hold all questions until I'm finished speaking." He spat on the floor. "I'll tell you what I can, just please don't hurt me again. We have a deal?" He sounded much more audible now.

Brent and Patrick didn't like the idea, but they had to put up with it. "Yes," they both replied.

"Good, now let me explain." Ken spat again and took a deep breath. "Brent: Your real name is David Webb-"Brent opened his mouth to ask something, but Ken answered his question before he even asked, "Yes, like Jason Bourne's name in the Bourne movies." Brent closed his mouth. The memories that flooded to Patrick a few minutes ago flew into Brent's mind now. All the occasions where people called Brent, "David" when he was younger were becoming vivid to him, and bits and pieces of random memories were being recollected, too.

"Patrick, your real name is Henry Bowman; no movie reference there. Now I bet that both of you want to know why your names were changed, and why you have no remembrance of this event, right?" Brent and Patrick slowly nodded. Ken put his hands behind his head and inhaled and exhaled deeply. "Well, here goes..." He began to sound muffled again, so he spat on the ground once more; his spit was almost all red. "I'm not actually a mechanical engineer, although this job, the car mechanic one, I do as a side job. I work for a company, whose name I shall not address, and one day, somehow two unknown peoples, that would be you two, walked in randomly and saw what we were doing. We couldn't have that, so we had to do something about it. We ended up knocking you both out and lobotomizing both of you, giving you fake names and fake memories in which to run from. That's why you both have that flower pedal-like scar on your skull lines. We gave you fake memories of it being a birth mark."

Brent and Patrick both rubbed their lobotomy scars, and felt the incision. Both shuttered after feeling the scar.

"Your names we made from my experiences with both of you. David, your favorite bands were Rise Against and Shinedown, so we combined Brent Smith's first name with Tim McIlrath's last name, and thus Brent McIlrath was born. Henry, your favorite bands were Fall Out Boy and Green Day, so we combined Patrick Stump with Billy Joe Armstrong, and then Patrick Armstrong was made. We were very elaborate in your memories; we created fake lives in which you both lived. David, we made you rich and have multiple trophies, servants, and pictures around your mansion so that you could believe that you were rich easier." Brent looked away at this and he looked absolutely destroyed. His face was blank and pale as could be. He stayed like this, motionless, for a little while.

"Now Henry, we made you poor, and, well you just sort of adopted the lifestyle with very little influence by my company." Henry, instead of looking away, glared at Ken. His fists, which were clenched to begin with, became even tighter.

"The reason we made one of you rich, and the other poor was to secure that neither of you would ever meet again. Evidently, you did and you are here…If I wouldn't have fucked up and said, 'Patrick', as opposed to, 'Henry', we might not have been having this conversation right now."

"And you'd have a few more teeth," Patrick said through his own gritted teeth. Ken seemed to disregard that comment, spat out more blood, and continued:

"Moreover, we planned around the idea that you two would never meet up again, seeing as most rich people aren't friends with poor fold, and vice versa." Ken paused and touched his face a bit. "This might be a dumb question, but do you two have any questions?" He looked at Patrick, then at Patrick's fists. "I'll…be willing to answer most questions, assuming I can answer them."

Brent just sat there, rather than asking anything. His eyes were blank, and his skin was pale, as if he had just seen a ghost. Hell, he was starting to think that he was a ghost. He stared down at his hands, and didn't move for a long time after that. He just sat, there, staring.

"I have a question for you, Ken?" spoke Patrick, "If what you're saying is true…"

Ken interjected with, "It is true."

"…right," Patrick continued, "If what you're saying is true, then what did we do that would require us to be lobotomized?"

"I'm afraid I can't tell you that, Henry," Ken said back. Patrick didn't like being called, "Henry". It didn't feel natural to him.

Brent, after a few minutes, finally looked up from his void that he's been staring into for the past while, and finally asked Ken a question.

"Ken, I have no questions for you." His voice was quiet and fierce, "I don't want to know anymore. I don't want to know who I thought I was, who I really am, or who I want, or wanted, to be." He considered Ken's eyes, and started tearing up a little, "I thought we were friends, but friends don't do this to one another." Ken looked away from Brent, and felt the guilt trip come on him, like a freight train riding on his shoulders, "I don't want to have to know, but I must." Brent sniffled, and looked up, looking serious and ready for action now. His hands were now clenched; shaking with rage and anticipation. "I want to find out on my own, not have some filthy, low-life bottom feeder tell me everything that I want to know, just so that *bastard*," he put heavy emphasis on the word, "bastard," as he looked deeper into Ken's eyes. Ken just shuttered. Brent continued, "Can tell me that he can't disclose that information, or else the company that he works for will give him verbal lashings. Not that I want to hear anything from this lying sack of shit anyways. However, I would like to know one thing and one thing only. I want to know, how much of our memories are true. What didn't you change about us? That should give me enough information to satisfy me, and hopefully Patrick as well."

Brent had always been good at making speeches. He could convince someone to do practically whatever he wants, using his words. He spoke so clean, so sincere, and so passionately that it was hard to not get caught in what he was saying. This effect usually worked on Ken as well, but Ken stayed quiet after Brent's speech.

Brent hit Ken as hard as he could with a clenched fist. Ken's head reared back, and then hung down low. After a few moments, Ken looked back up and said, "The things that we didn't change about you, or at least tried to change but your guys' minds just wouldn't have it, are as follows. Your personalities; they stayed the same. Both of your loves for music; they stayed the same. Your physical structures and looks; they stayed the same as well. Your mental thought processes, which honestly we should have changed," he said that last part under his breath, "both stayed the same, in addition to everything else I mentioned." Your friends, and recollections of them, all of those are true. Such as the recollections that we just went through, right before…" Ken looked again at Brent and Patrick, then shut himself up before going any further. "Right. Well, your friends have remained untouched."

"So, all our friends that we can recall, they haven't been tampered with?" Patrick asked.

"As far as I'm aware, no they have not been messed with."

"I assume that our memories of you weren't tampered with, either?" Patrick queried.

"You're a smart one, Henry." Ken chuckled, and then coughed heavily. "I'm trying to think of other things that we didn't change…but I can't think of anymore. So that's either all of them, or I purposely forgot the other ones in case a moment such as this were to happen. So, hope that the information I gave you two helps."

Brent, being silent throughout Patrick and Ken's conversation, began to animate once more. He's been thinking about what to say to Ken next; the next round of belligerent speech.

"I love how you say, 'We were friends when we were younger.' However, I don't consider you my friend."

"Oh God, here we go again…" thought Ken, when Brent started to speak again.

Brent continued to say, starting to look up and towards Ken again:

"A friend would have stuck up for us back…how long ago were we lobotomized?"

"Seven years ago; 2005 to be exact." Ken replied, very quickly.

"Thank you; a friend would have stuck up for us back in 2005, but you didn't. You, from what it seems to be, almost sound to be a conspirator for what happened." Ken's eyes quickly darted to the floor after this comment. "But I'll give you a break on what being a friend means; there's a dictionary for that. After what you've told us today, I've lost all respect for you." Patrick nodded with this remark, screaming for joy on the inside, "I don't feel as if I could say anything to you, and expect you to keep it a secret.

"With all that said, however, I do require something of you, Ken. The reason I came to this shop in the first place was because my…I don't think it's even my limo anymore…anyway, my limo broke down and I came here to see if you could help me see what's wrong with it and fix it up. My limo driver already called a tow truck; he should be here soon. So, could you please do this for me, to make up for what horrible things you've done to Patrick and me?"

"Yes," Ken replied, "I'll gladly fix your limo for you. I've felt horrible about what I've done, don't get me wrong, I've regretted it as soon as I casted my vote to lobotomize you two. I'm not lyin', either; I really have. I know that nothing that I ever do, or can do for you two, can ever make up for what I've done to your lives. You can hate me all you want, in fact I want you too, and I encourage it. So, I will gladly fix up your limo for you. It's the least I can do."

"Well I appreciate it, and your thoughts, Ken. I will take them with a grain of salt." Brent stood up. "Patrick, let's go."

"Agreed." Patrick then stood up as well. The two walked away from Ken and the foldable chairs they were sitting in. As they were walking away from the scene of the bad news, they heard Ken exclaim, from behind them:

"Wait!" He stood up from his stool and hobbled over to Brent and Patrick; he almost tripped a few times along the way. "I have one last thing I need to say. If you two do end up deciding to find out more about what happened to you, then this should be helpful to you two. If someone calls you, 'Brent', or, 'Patrick', then that's an easy giveaway that they know what has happened with you. Now how you treat the people that reply with that is up to you. Conversely, the people who call you, 'David', or, 'Henry' most likely don't know what's happened to you two over the past few years. I just thought that I would bring that to both of your attentions. Take that information as you will; it's something that I feel obligated to tell you."

Patrick replied, "Well thank you, Ken. We will use that if we decide to go around the country, trying to find out what happened…" Patrick said this very sarcastically. Brent and Patrick then, leaving their innocence behind, walked away from Ken, his car, the radio, the chairs that lay in their triangular formation, and the cold room that didn't help calm the nerves of Brent and Patrick. They then continued out into the lobby, not looking at Pam as they walked through the room, and opened the door as they let the warmth of the sun overcome their senses and their thoughts; even if it was only for a moment.

Chapter 8

Soon after reentering the sun lit outside world, Brent and Patrick's ears readjusted to the sound of multiple people speaking at once, sounding monotone as they did, and the sound of cars that whizzed past them every so often. The longer they stood there, the more their thoughts started to get to them, and the conversation they just had with Ken started to make sense to them.

"Hey, Patrick…or, I guess I should say, Henry," Brent turned and said to Patrick/Henry, "I know we both have a lot to think about, and you're starting to think about what just happened, as am I, but let's try and not do that; at least right now. I'm starving, and I assume that you are too, being poor and all, so how about we go out to lunch; my treat. I was thinking that we could also talk about what just happened at lunch, too."

"No. No, no ,no. I don't want to be any more of a burden than I am now…" Patrick started to say, waving his hands around in front of him as sort of a visual show.

"No, you won't be any form of a burden, my friend. Or, at least I think you are my friend…" Brent scratched his lobotomy scar after saying that.

"If you say so," Patrick said, sighing in the process, "So where are we going?" Patrick asked this while Brent was starting to move to the left of the shop, leaving it behind. Patrick sprinted forward to catch up with Brent, not that he had to sprint, mind you.

"I was thinking Outback Steakhouse; I was planning on going out to lunch today after I met up with Jaime, but seeing as it's…" Brent checked his phone. In doing so, he also quickly glanced at the date. It read November 22nd, 2012. "1:25PM, I figured I might as well eat now. I don't have an appointment with Jaime, it's just whenever I show up is when we meet." It got quiet for a few seconds, and both Patrick and Brent's minds started to flood with thoughts once more. Brent interrupted both men's thoughts again.

"Oh, and just so you know, Patrick, you can order whatever you like at Outback. Considering I'm rich, with what I assume is probably blood money, there's no harm in ordering whatever you like."

"Anything, huh?" Patrick's mind started to rush with thoughts of food, and what to order at Outback. His mouth started to water. Brent's mind, however, went back to how hungry he was, and he was hoping to get to Outback soon. It was about a 5-minute walk from "Heavy Metal", but it felt much longer in his own mind. From this conversation about food, however, Brent and Patrick forgot about what happened just moments ago, or at least for a while they did.

Arriving at the Outback Steakhouse, they walked in and the hostess led the two men to their seats, which was near the back of the restaurant, and to a booth that was indented into the wall. Moments after being seated, their waitress walked by and took their orders. Both men already made up their minds for as to what they wanted prior to walking into the restaurant. Both ordered the same thing, coincidentally. They ordered the 9oz Outback Special, medium-well, with a side orders consisting of a baked potato and green beans. To drink, Brent and Patrick both ordered Pepsi. They ordered the drink to come with the meal; they wanted nothing to drink while they were talking about what to do next.

As the lady walked away, Brent leaned in towards Patrick, who sat on the opposite side of the booth they were given to sit in, and began to speak.

"OK, so let's just jump right into what just happened back there. I have a question: Should we continue to call each other Brent and Patrick, or David and Henry, respectively?"

"I personally would rather be called Patrick; it feels more natural to me. Plus, when Ken called me Henry, it felt awkward. So, I cast my vote towards Brent and Patrick."

Patrick replied, trying the pepper and salt grinders on the tables, and watching them fall onto a nearby napkin.

"OK, so then it's settled. Brent and Patrick, it is. Personally, I preferred that, too." Brent cracked his knuckles, for he did this every once and a while, before he was about to ask something, or say something. Not always, though; just whenever he thought about it. "Maybe it's just me, but I never thought about our 'fake' names being named after our favorite artists. I mean, you'd think it would be pretty obvious."

"Eh, maybe for you," Patrick said, as he stopped grinding the salt and pepper, and placed the grinders back down in their respective areas. "I never thought of it, because my name actually sounds real. Yours…while I never thought of the possibility either, it does sound a bit more out of place then my name." Patrick sounded as if he was holding something back, and Brent could feel it, but he decided not to press Patrick. He figured that they would probably end up getting around to what ails Patrick eventually.

"Yeah…I guess so…" Brent replied, covertly.

Patrick started to giggle a little bit. "It's odd, when Ken said, 'Henry' all these memories started coming back to me…instantaneously, too. There was no real rhyme or reason behind them; they just kinda appeared there."

"You know, I felt something like that," Brent interjected. "Memories started to come back to me, too. Most of them weren't even full memories; just bits and pieces…" Brent paused and looked around for a moment. He then leaned in close to Patrick and said quietly, "Hey, wouldn't it be funny, if someone just randomly were to walk by us when we were having this conversation?"

"Yeah, they'd just look at us and think, 'What's wrong with those guys? Fake names? Real names? What kind of drugs are they on…'" Brent said this with a very funny old man accent. They both had a good laugh over the impression alone.

While the two were still chuckling over the impression, their waitress walked by their table, stopped in front of the men and handed them their bread and butter, which was complimentary of Outback Steakhouse to do. She also handed them two plates, which were warm to the touch.

As the waitress walked away, Brent pulled out his knife from inside his napkin and cut the bread into fourths. Brent took one piece of the bread, put it onto his warm plate, and used the knife to spread butter all over the bread. Patrick, however, wasn't being as diligent as Brent was with his food. Patrick just nabbed the three remaining pieces of bread and shoved them all down his throat. It was quite a disgusting sight to see.

After Brent finished eating his bread diligently, and Patrick finished eating his bread like a monster, Patrick wiped his mouth with his salt and pepper filled napkin. To be honest, it wasn't a very well thought out idea. He ended up spitting out the contents of salt and pepper, and traces of bread all over the table. Instead of being irritated, or annoyed by this, Brent just laughed at the sight of the pitiful Patrick.

After Patrick correctly wiped his mouth of the contents around his mouth, he started to ask Brent a question.

"Say," his voice sounded very gruff for some reason. He coughed to eliminate the sound. "I know what we both are really wondering about..."

"Here's what I was talking about earlier..." Brent thought to himself, while Patrick started off his topic.

"We both want to know about who we really are. Who exactly are we? I don't know, and I know you don't. But do we really want to know?"

"What do you mean by that?" Brent asked.

"I mean, do we really want to try and find out who we really are?"

"Oh...I don't know. I mean, I guess we sort of have to find out..."

"But that's what I'm trying to say," Patrick sounded kind of irritated by this point, "We could just as easily take Ken's words as fact, just as much as we would a joke. He always joked around with us when we were younger, so who's to say that he's no different now, and that he's just fabricating this for a huge prank, or something?"

Brent started to think it over. "Well, I still don't know...I need some time to think about this..."

"We don't have time to think!" Patrick practically shouted this. Some people sitting in seats near Brent and Patrick's booth looked over to see what the big deal was, but they turned their heads away almost as quickly as they turned their heads towards the two. "This choice only affects two people right now; me and you." He pointed at Brent with his index finger.

"Get that finger away from me," Brent said, coldly, as he pushed Patrick's finger off to the side. "It's true that Ken has always been a trickster. And yes, this could all just be a prank, on a much larger scale, mind you. But...I just don't know about this. I've never seen him this sincere and focused about something ever before; it's rather perplexing. Plus, like you said, I just...felt something when he said 'David'. Something clicked in my head. I can't explain it very well, but I get this feeling that this might be real."

Patrick was quiet for a little bit before finally grunting and muttering, "Look," Patrick paused. "To be honest, and I've never told you this before, but I've never really liked, or better yet trusted Ken; ever. In fact, I've always kinda hated him." Brent looked as if he rejected this news. "But I never told you this, in hopes that our friendship could stay intact. I never planned on telling you this information, but I thought now would be a good time to get it from my chest. Sorry if it troubles you, but considering what news we both received today, I think you can manage."

"Oh no, I understand. In fact, I thought you like this for a while now," Brent said, in a sarcastic tone. Patrick looked misled by this. "I understand, totally. You never trusted him, but now that it's come to my attention you like to rub it in my face."

"No, I didn't mean it like that..." Patrick was cut off.

"I know; I was wrong about Ken. I should have caught on like you did way back when, is that what you want me to say? That I'm wrong, and you're right? If that's the case, I will. I, Brent McIlrath, was wrong about Ken Sinclair. This man, Patrick Armstrong, was right all along. I should have known-"

"Will you just shut the fuck up?" Patrick leaned over the table and grabbed Brent by the collar of his suit. Brent gulped. Very quietly, Patrick added, "That was not my intention. I was just trying to say that I haven't trusted him, and this today hasn't helped his reputation with me. Now calm the hell down. We need to talk about this in a more serious manner." Patrick released Brent, and Patrick slumped back down into his seat in the booth. Brent leaned backward, too, and fixed his suit collar. He dared not to look at Patrick now. "I mean, Jesus Christ," Patrick continued, "Ever since the incident with Ken you've been acting like a completely different person."

"That's because I might be a completely different person." Brent said, very held back. He still wasn't looking at Patrick when he said this.

"And that's what we need to talk about." Patrick put his hands together on the words, "that's", "need" and "talk." "Should we pursue this idea that we are people that we don't know about, and assume that everything we know is a lie? Or should we just move on with our lives, and just think of Ken's words as nothing? Meaningless."

Brent finally looked back up at Patrick. *"Good, I got through to him."* Patrick thought. He continued, "I personally think that we shouldn't trust Ken. I think he's a no-good scumbag, whose words can't be taken seriously. But that's just my opinion; Brent, I need some input here, come on." Patrick snapped his fingers a few times.

Brent replied, "Listen, I'm sorry that I've been such an asshole to you. It's just that...the whole situation that we've been put in...it's unsettling. There are so many, 'What if?' factors in it that it's hard to distinguish fiction from reality. I personally think that, yes while I don't think we should trust what Ken told us, what if he was telling the truth? What if he's not just pranking us and those scars on our foreheads aren't just birthmarks, and they are actual lobotomy scars? I say that we give his words a chance to live. I'm going to go see Jaime after we're done eating anyway and I encourage that you come along with me. After I'm done talking to him with what we need to talk about, I'm going to ask him about the incident.

If he seems like he knows nothing about it, then I'll move on with the rest of my life. If there's even the smallest doubt that something could be going on, then I'll press him and get some answers out of him, whether they end up going cold or turning up hot.

"Now, whether you end up deciding to come with me or not, I'm going to follow through with what I just said. You can either join me and go through whatever could happen, and we'll figure it out from there, or you can walk away with what little you have now and always ask yourself for the rest of your life, 'What if?' The choice is yours, my friend. Now what will it be?"

"Well with a speech like that, who could say no? I'm in." Patrick put his hand out into the air, and about halfway across the table. Brent soon put his hand on top of Patrick's. This hand-on-hand action soon traversed into a handshake. After the two men had finished their trust handshake, the waitress arrived with their food. She laid down the plates in front of Brent and Patrick, and walked away to get the drinks. She returned bearing the drinks in her hands, as well as the bill for their meal. Brent and Patrick took no time in waiting for their drinks, and started devouring, yet still savoring the food that was placed in front of them, almost immediately. It was the best and worst meal Brent and Patrick had ever eaten in their entire lives.

Chapter 9

-Ignorance; Paramore-

Upon finishing their meal, Brent paid the bill and the two got up from their booths and left the restaurant. Some people looked at the two as they walked by them to get to the door. Seeing as what just happened between the two of them, they thought that they can stare all they want. Besides, both highly doubted they would ever see any of them again.

Walking outside of the restaurant, Brent and Patrick turned left, and headed back towards the direction of "Heavy Metal"; Jaime's shop was in that direction, at the very end of Midway Street. You see, Midway Street is the longest street in Preston, Oklahoma, because it exceeds south by the longest amount, and then the road turns to the east and heads that way until it reaches about the end of Main Street, but it doesn't connect with Main street; it's hard to explain without looking at a map. Regardless, Jaime's shop lies at the very end of Midway Street.

On their way down to the shop, Brent's pocket started to vibrate. It, at first, startled Brent, but then he realized within a millisecond that it was his phone going off. He pulled it out of his phone, and Brent, Patrick, and anyone within a mile radius could hear Brent's loud ringtone; it played "Amaryllis" by Shinedown. As he checked the caller ID, the lyrics of the song could be clearly identified. Patrick was enjoying the song, but then it was cut off when Brent answered the phone. Patrick felt a little sad on the inside. Patrick, hearing only Brent's side of the conversation, listened to the conversation, or at least as much of it that he could.

"Hello? Oh, hey, S! OK, cool....Alright....OK....Hey, listen, if you want to, you can go ahead and get yourself something to eat. I'll pay you back the money later....Yeah.....No problem!.....Thanks for everything, S! You're the best....Ha-ha....OK, now. Bye." Brent hung up.

"Who was that?" queried Patrick.

"Oh, yes, I forgot to tell you about him. I just got off the phone with my limo driver, S."

"You have a limo, AND a limo driver? Ahh, that's so awesome!" Brent tried to hold back a smile. "But now I'm getting besides myself; why do you call him 'S'?"

"You know, that's a great question, because I don't know the answer to that one," Brent said, laughing as he did. He and Patrick kept walking forward at a semi-brisk pace. "His real name is Samuel, but I don't know. I don't remember when, or how, but I ended up calling him 'S' and it just…stuck, I guess. Maybe that could be one of those memories that was implanted in me, so that's why I can't remember it, but…" Brent stopped himself.

"Well, since I'm curious now," Patrick started to say, "Who else works for you, since I assume you have some form of maintenance to run that mansion of yours."

", not a whole lot of people, to be honest. There's Mrs. Green, who is our cook, Mrs. Bayer, who is one of our two maids, Mr. Nash, Mr. Seitz, Mr. Rose, and Mrs. Laudinsky, all four of which man the "tollbooth", as we like to call it, which operates the gate leading to and from my mansion. There's also S, whom I've already explained, and the last one, and my newest recruit, is Ms. Fisher…" Brent seemed to space-out when he uttered Ms. Fisher's name. Patrick knew something was up with that. Patrick looked over to his right and saw the sign, "Heavy Metal" above Ken's shop. Patrick tried not to think of him.

"Hey, hey! Ground control to Major Brent! Earth doesn't want you gone…yet." Brent shook himself out of his delusion. "I have two questions about what you've told me. One: Why did you say everyone's name with a 'Mr.', 'Mrs.', or 'Ms.'?"

"Well," Brent said as he was thinking of what to say next, "that's because I like to keep things formal back at the mansion. I'd like to prefer to everyone as a 'Mr.', 'Mrs.', or 'Ms.', as I would like to be called Mr. McIlrath. I have a great boss-worker relationship with all my workers," Patrick rolled his eyes at this; Brent didn't notice and went on, "so I could call them by their first names, but I just don't. Well, I call S by his nickname, but that doesn't really count. Now what was your second question?

"As yes, my second question," Patrick started to ask, "is what's up with you and Ms. Fisher-does she have a name? I feel weird saying Ms., considering I don't know who she is."

"Her full name is Hannah Fisher, just so you know. And what do you mean, 'up with you and Ms. Fisher'?"

"You did that thing that you do."

Brent looked confused.

"What thing?"

"You know, that thing that you do whenever you have a case of the 'girl crazy'." Patrick was starting to wonder if Brent knew what he was talking about.

"I have no clue what you're talking about." Brent quickly said back. That cleared up Patrick's suspicion.

"Oh, you know. Whenever you are all over a girl you start to space-out when you say her name. You did this with Cassidy in 8th grade, and again with Erika when we were sophomores. Those are the only two girls I can remember off-hand, but those are examples. And to me it looks like you're doing it with this, 'Hannah' girl, too."

Brent sighed. He and Patrick crossed a crosswalk, and then headed left; the street forced them to go that way. Brent suddenly was reminded of Cassidy and Erika from when he was younger. Brent put his hands in his pockets, and continued to strut forward.

"Fine. You caught me red handed; I think I like my newest maid, Hannah. But, I don't know if I like her enough yet. So, I'm not going to just waltz up to her and ask her out like I did with Cassidy and Erika. I've grown up a bit since then."

"Albeit not much?" Patrick smiled with his morbid humor.

"Oh, shut up." Patrick laughed at that comeback from Brent. Brent went on, "Anyway, don't bring this fact up to her if you see her, OK? I'd like to keep this on the down low, if at least for a while."

"You can count on me." Patrick put his left hand in the air, and his right hand on his chest.

"Now I want to go ahead and ask you a personal question, Patrick," Brent started off saying, "If you don't mind me asking, could you tell me about what's been going on with your family? Like, in detail?

"My family? Oh God, where do I begin? Also, I'm fine with speaking about it, so don't you worry. Oh man…now, since I'm not totally sure if what I remember of them is true or not, go ahead and jump in now and again to keep me on track, you hear?" He turned his attention towards Brent.

"Yeah, sure thing. I was going to do it anyway, but now I have permission; thanks," he said jokingly.

"A-ha. Well, let's just go through all my memories of my family. My mother, Misty, was, and as far as I'm concerned, is still a drunkard. She was always disillusioned and never really looked out for me, my sister, or my brother. In fact, I don't think she even really raised us. It was my father who always stepped in and did the heavy lifting; going to our dance recitals, musicals, school events, what have you. This coming in true so far?" he asked Brent.

"Yep. As far as I remember, this seems to be accurate."

"OK, good. I guess this is all true then…which is more sad than good, but I digress. My father, Gary, seemed to be the only sane one in our family. Like I said, he always showed up to our activities and cheered us on, even if we weren't doing well. I'm not sure about my other siblings, but he taught me right from wrong, how to be polite, the effect that being kind and respectful can have on someone, you know, things that both parents should have done. It only made things worse whenever he and my mother got divorced about a year before I left the house." Patrick looked up into the sky, seeing if there were any clouds up there. There wasn't; the sky was clear of any white markings.

"From that point on," he continued, "my mother went on drunken rampages almost every night, and our income started to dwindle. We were mostly living off what little money I could earn, by the way I worked at a Save-A-Lot as a bagger, but quit once my new boss came in and started upping the hours and lowering the pay." Brent shook his head to Patrick's words, showing him that so far, his memories haven't deceived him.

Patrick kept going, "My brother and sister also offered up money to support the family, or at least whatever they could afford to contribute. It seemed as if whenever my dad left, everything started to go downhill. My younger sister, Holly, whom if I remember right, had a serious drug addiction. She always had a drug problem, even when my father was around, but it wasn't as bad. It was, like, a cigarette here, a cigarette there, every once and a while she would binge on cocaine and heroin, weed sometimes as well. But my father (not to mention some of his police buddies) always ended up helping my sister off her problem, at least for a while. Once my father left though, her problems seemed to get too far out of control. Her drug problems were one of the big influences for as to why I left the house, but that's a different story for a different day. She also was very…well, cracked I guess is a good word to use. She went insane about the same time she graduated High School, in 2005. After she graduated, she started to worry about what to do with her life. So, in turn, she tried to calm her mind, let alone deal with stress, by doing drugs. My dad was still around at that time, though he left that same year; that's why she was granted her pot smoking privileges, because our mother didn't give two shits, and Holly wouldn't listen to what my brother nor what I said to her. She contemplated suicide a few times, and even attempted it as well. This included slitting her wrists, almost shooting herself in the head with a gun, stabbing herself with a steak knife, etc. I was almost always the one to talk her out of taking her life, with my brother having to do it once or twice, if I'm recalling correctly. Do you remember most of this?"

"Yes, I do." Brent held his head low, feeling sorry for Patrick and his life. "Well, if I remember this, then that means that this must all be true as well, huh?"

"I guess so," he sighed. Looking pained, as if someone just stabbed him. He continued his story: "This all happened when I was about 20 years old, and we've been separated for 7 years, so I'm going to assume this all occurred before out lobotomies. While my sister and mother stayed home, getting either high or drunk off their asses, my older brother, Matt, went away to college on a football scholarship."

"Well good for him!" Brent said, seeing that maybe Patrick's story would start to become sort of happy. "Yeah, I remember him leaving for college when we were seniors. He was a year older than you, right?"

"Yes, he was and still is."

"So, what did he major in, do you know? I don't remember you ever telling me this when we were younger." Brent said.

"Well that could mean that what I'm about to say could be a figment of the fake memories," Patrick looked to be kind of saddened by this news. Patrick went on, "He majored in Law, and ended up becoming a lawyer. 'Matt Armstrong, Attorney at Law. Saving you from further injuries to your wallet.' That's his slogan. You can see signs of his propaganda all over this town, if you look in all the right places."

"Well, it sounds like it can't be augmented, seeing as his signs are all over town." Brent contradicted Patrick.

"Yes, but do you think that the company that lobotomized us could have arranged his life style to fit the needs of ours?" Patrick retorted.

"I guess that would be a possibility." Brent said, as he realized that he probably sounded dumb in Patrick's eyes. Brent decided to move past that and wanted to hear what Patrick had to say about Matt, "Well at least it sounds like he's doing well in life! I thought you said that everything went downhill?" Brent pondered.

"Oh, I haven't gotten to his problem yet," Patrick began, "I talked to him via a payphone a while ago, and he told me that he hates his job; to the very core. All he does is lie for people that he knows have done bad things. It kills him on the inside. Every once in a blue moon he'll get someone who is telling the truth about not committing a crime, or something along that nature. He loves helping those people, but those stories are few and far between. Most every other day he deals with idiots who don't know a judge from a prosecutor. When I still lived at home, I had to hear about it every day when he came home, about, 'I hate this job so much. These people only want me to help their selves try to get money from tax companies; every damn day! I'm sick of it! I'm moving out of this house and I'm going to change my major!' He moved out of the house, eventually, but he still hasn't changed his career. It's sad to think about him. I mean, yeah, the money he makes gives him a good living, but overall it's just not worth it, it seems." He paused and added, "I'd rather be poor than do what he's doing, honestly…"

Trying to forget about the subject matter entirely, Patrick looked up and to his right and saw a fancy looking store. It had glass windows, and black frames. Its theme was a retro/futuristic look. He saw a secretary sitting behind a desk inside of the windowed room, surrounded by a TV, and two chairs facing the TV inside of the lobby. The TV was off, and the chairs were unoccupied now. The secretary looked to be an older woman, whom was writing something down on a sheet of paper.

"Well, this is the place," said Brent, looking up at the sign of the store. Patrick looked up at the sign in unison. "Jaime's Wood" read the sign. The two men started to act like little kids again, since the sign read "Wood." They chuckled as if they were 20 years younger again, and for a moment forgot about who they really are, or who they really could be.

"I've known that this place was called 'Jaime's Wood' for a while now, but every time I hear about the name, or see it, it still cracks me up." Brent said, still chuckling.

"I'm laughing more at the fact that he named the place this! If he didn't do this on purpose, then I don't want to know how he didn't notice that?" Patrick said, still grinning and laughing.

After the two stopped laughing, Brent broke out and said, "God, we're seven-year-olds again…" Patrick just smiled back to this. Brent and Patrick then entered Jaime's place of business, opening the glass doors that separated the outside world from the controlled biome of the inside.

Upon entering the lobby of "Jaime's Wood", Brent and Patrick were greeted by an elderly secretary, whom looked up at the sound of the creaking door. "May I help you two?" she cried out.

"Yes," said Brent, stepping closer towards the desk that the secretary sought shelter behind. The secretary was an elderly woman, who looked to be about 60 years-old, or so. Her hair was thin and tied back, and she had wrinkles all over her face. Her lips were red with lipstick. She wore a pearl necklace on her neck, and she was wearing a blue shirt with a dark blue jacket over top of the shirt. She wore no nametag of any sort, setting her apart from the secretary of Ken's business. Brent, still observing the woman, continued to speak, "I was wondering if we could see Mr. Belcher."

"Do you have an appointment?" the secretary asked.

"Yes, well technically. My appointment was set up to where I could show up at any point in the day, before closing time."

The secretary looked at her appointments list, with a pen in here hand. She laid the pen next to the first name on the list. "Name, please."

"Oh, yes. Sorry. McIlrath, Brent."

She moved her hand down the paper. Slowly she checked each name, to make sure she didn't miss anything. Brent peered over the desk to watch her as she moved her hand down the list. About halfway down the paper, her hand shifted from going down vertically, to moving to the right horizontally. Brent saw that is was his name that she found. He glanced at the name before his, which read, "George Butler". His appointment slot was filled out and read, "14:30". Military time. *"Why does someone have an appointment time? Mrs. Green told me he was free all day...!"* Brent thought to himself. He eventually chalked it up to, *"He must have walked in on short-notice, or something.* "The woman's hand stopped when she hovered over to the appointment time slot. It read, "SPECIAL". To her that meant something, as she said, "Alright. Mr. Belcher is actually with someone at the current moment." She paused, and turned her attention over to

Patrick. She darted her eyes back to Brent. "He with you?" she asked him.

"Yes, ma'am, he is."

"I was just making sure. You two will have to wait until Mr. Belcher's company has left. You sit on those chairs while you wait, if you would like." She pointed over towards a few chairs which were facing the TV; adjacent to the desk. Brent and Patrick turned around, and started walking towards the chairs. The secretary went back to writing down things on her paper.

As Brent and Patrick sat down, they noticed how broken down and uncomfortable the chairs were. It was nothing they couldn't handle, it was just annoying. Brent looked around the room, and found a wall clock on the wall that was farthest away from Brent and Patrick. He read the time off the clock. "2:45PM." Brent thought to himself, *"Ugh. That 'George' guy just got in there. It might take him a while to leave, too. I guess we'll just sit here and wait then..."*

Brent could have pulled out his phone and did something, either texting someone or calling the mansion to see how things were going. He could have even played a game if he wanted, but he knew that Patrick didn't have a phone of any sort, so he decided that he would suffer through the boredom with Patrick.

Patrick was twiddling his thumbs, and staring into the darkness that the TV provided when it was turned off. Brent decided to join Patrick in watching the greatest TV program ever: "Nothing." Although, it wasn't completely blackened out, the TV screen that is. Brent and Patrick could see their reflections in the screen. As they looked at each other through the screen, they thought about what their plan of action would be for when they see Jaime and ask him about their memories. They can either find out Ken was just pulling a prank on them, and then they had a few options:

    A.)   They could go to Ken and beat him up

          a.   Then go on with their lives, and Brent and Patrick still be friends

          b.   Then go on with their lives, and Brent and Patrick never see each other again.

B.) Leave Ken alone.
  a. Brent and Patrick could continue to be friends
  b. Brent and Patrick could stop being friends and never see each other again.
C.) Pull a prank on Ken to get back at him.
  a. Brent and Patrick stay friends.
  b. Brent and Patrick stop being friends and never see each other again.

On the other hand, they could walk out of Jaime's business and could learn that Ken was telling the truth, and then the possibilities were endless. Brent and Patrick both, secretly, tried deciphering some of the possibilities in their own separate minds. Brent and Patrick then stopped focusing on what they saw in the reflection of the TV, but more on what was going on in their minds. They sat like this, and did this, until Jaime's client walked out of the store, and the secretary called the two up to meet with Jaime.

"Brent and company!" yelled the secretary, "You may now go speak with Jaime." Brent and Patrick snapped out of their fake little worlds and awoke back into reality. They stood up from the chairs, which they forgot how uncomfortable they were, and walked past the secretary's desk to get into Jaime's room. The secretary stopped them.

"I almost forgot. Jaime is the last door down the hallway. Just keep going straight, and you should be good." She went back to writing. Brent tried to look over at what she was doing as he walked past her, but he couldn't catch a glimpse.

Walking down the hallway, Brent and Patrick looked at the names on the doors as they walked past them. "Jonathan Steele", "Robert Moore", "Carrie Swayer", "Bruce White", and "Michelle Green" were the names they saw in gold platting on all the doors the two walked past. After a little while, Brent and Patrick reached the last door, which read, "Jaime Belcher". Brent knocked on the door, and heard a faint, "Come in." He opened the door, and Patrick and he filed into the room.

Chapter 10

-Architects; Rise Against-

Brent closed the door behind him as he and Patrick slid on through the doorway. The found themselves looking at Jaime Belcher, who sat behind his desk which was cluttered with papers and blueprints that he was looking at. The front of his desk sat a desk name plate, which had Jaime's name engraved into it. One of the other things that Brent and Patrick noticed almost immediately was a 6 or 7-inch-tall cross, which had a figure of Jesus nailed to the cross. Jesus seemed to be hunched over on the cross; it looked like he was trying to escape the clutches of the nails through his hands and feet, but to no avail. For some reason, Brent found this decoration to be a little unnerving. Behind Jaime's desk was a huge glass window pane which overlooked a forest that lay behind Jaime's store, apparently.

Jaime looked up from his blueprints to see Brent and Patrick standing there, looking back at him.

"Oh, well hello Day-uh, Brent!" he cleared his throat. Brent and Patrick both heard this and exchanged unsure looks. Brent felt his heart begin to beat faster. Jaime went on, "And why hello to you too, Patrick! I didn't expect to see you here!" Jaime stood up to shake hands with the two men from his past. "Sorry about not being all dressed up; I was out working in the field this morning, so I just wore clothes that fit accordingly to that."

Jaime wore a plaid red and white shirt, and normal looking blue jeans. His shirt had a pocket on it, which held what looked to be drawing tools in it. He wore glasses and his brown hair was combed back to make him look more professional. Jaime was a little chubby, but not enough that anyone would really notice it; Jaime was just about as tall as Brent.

Brent and Patrick shook hands with the man, and when they were done, Brent and Patrick looked at each other with uncertainty in their eyes. Patrick decided that he wouldn't speak unless directly asked something; Brent was probably better off doing all the talking anyways.

"Please, take a seat." Jaime, after saying that, reclined back into his own chair. Brent and Patrick sat down in unison. They felt much more comfortable in these seats than in the ones which rested in the lobby. These had arm rests and everything. "Wait, actually," Jaime started, "would one of you mind flipping the light switch on the wall, please? It's starting to get a little dark out now."

Patrick stood up and walked a few paces behind where he was sitting. He flipped the switch, and light illuminated the room. Patrick didn't even notice how dark the room was until he turned on the lights. He sat back down in his chair immediately after turning on the lights.

"So how are you two doing?" asked Jaime, as he started to clear his desk of his miscellaneous materials.

"Good," replied Brent.

"Fine," replied Patrick. He didn't want to mention the fact that he was homeless; he didn't want to stay longer than he had too.

"Well that's good to hear! So, Brent, I don't mean to be rude, but why is Patrick here?" Jaime asked, with a concerned look drawn on his face.

Brent thought up a semi-lie on-the-spot. "Well, I ran into him this morning, and I figured that you two haven't seen each other in quite some time, so I thought that he could tag along with me. That way you can see that he's not dead, or something like that."

"Oh, I wasn't complaining, mind you," Jaime said, trying to rationalize his question, "I was just wondering why he was here, is all."

"I understand," said Brent. He looked over at Patrick, and Patrick looked back at Brent with a questionable look on his face. Brent's heart began to beat a little bit faster now. "So, Jaime, how have you and your girlfriend, Acacia, been? I heard you two got married about two years ago. That true?"

"Yes sir, it is." Jaime held up his right hand, in which a ring sat on his ring finger. "Sorry about not inviting you two to the wedding. We wanted to keep it kind of a secret, so we only invited our immediate family members to it."

"Nah, it's cool. I get it," Brent said. "So, how's the marriage been turning out so far?"

"Good; really good, actually! I'm about to throw a bombshell at you two, but..." Jaime paused to build up anticipation, "Acacia is five months pregnant!"

"Really?" Brent exclaimed. Patrick looked shocked; excited too. He didn't say it, but his face did all the talking for him. Brent continued on to say, "Well good for you two! Make sure to send me some pics of the baby!"

"Trust me," Jaime said, "I will. I'll be flaunting that baby everywhere I go. I'm just so happy about being a father, you know." Jaime looked around on his desk, as if he was looking for something.

"Well, anyways, let's get on the topic of why I'm here." Brent seemed eager to get through this.

"Oh yes. Sorry, I got a bit too excited. Anyway, yes, about your addition," Jaime adjusted himself in his seat as he said this. He opened one of his drawers and took out a blueprint and uncoiled it on his desk, placing a few items on the corners to keep it from coiling itself once more, one of which was the cross. "You said you wanted to add a recreational room here; correct?" Jaime pointed to the area that was leading from the main room and connecting to the trophy room.

"Yes, I did; and I wanted it there, yes," Brent replied. The room also had dimensions on the outsides of the lines, which were supposed to indicate the walls. They were written in a form of gibberish that both Brent and Patrick could not read, and only architects seemed to understand what it said, or at least, that was Brent's philosophy.

"So, what did you say you wanted to use it for, again?" asked Jaime.

"Well, I kind of want it for multiple uses," began Brent, "Mainly I wanted to use it as a sort of room where all of my workers could go at the end of the day and hang out, and just relieve some stress. I wanted to add in a bowling alley, so that way my workers and I could all bowl some nights, and have a good time. Personally, I think I have a strong friendship with all my workers, except maybe Ms. Fisher, my newest recruit. I haven't gotten to know her very well, but I'm pretty sure that we'll get along just fine…" He smiled when he said that.

"Right…" Jaime looked as if he didn't believe Brent, but he never said it out loud. Brent paid no attention to Jaime's reaction, since he was away in la-la land, but Patrick took note of Jaime's reaction. Patrick adjusted in his seat as Jaime continued, "Well, anyways, Brent, when do you want me to come by and have my men start to work on constructing your addition?"

"Depends; how long will it take?" Brent asked. No longer was he in la-la land.

"For this type of addition, it would probably take us about 6 weeks to get just the build of the room done. If you want us to add the bowling alley into it, then that would probably take about 4 weeks, give or take a few. So, overall, it would be about 10 weeks, or so."

"OK," Brent thought about it for a moment or two, "Would this weekend work to break ground?"

Jaime looked at his calendar, which was attached to the desk, and sat under the blueprints. He pulled up the blueprints and looked at his calendar.

"Nope, sorry."

"Well," Brent got to thinking again, "How's about next Saturday?"

Jaime looked at his calendar again. He flipped the calendar over from November and looked at the first week of December. The date for next Saturday would be December 1st.

"That works for me, yes. So, are we agreeing upon next Saturday, then?" Jaime opened a drawer and pulled out a pencil from the compartment; the pencil was sharpened to a point. He put his hand down next to December 1st, and was awaiting Brent's answer.

"I guess so; next Saturday it is." Jaime then began to write down Brent's name on December 1st. He started to write something else down next to his name, but he then erased what he was writing and wrote over his original markings. He then put the November sheet overtop of the December sheet and put the blueprints as his top priority on his desk. "OK, so that's that! We'll talk about the price later, since I don't know an exact number as of now."

"Don't sweat it; money is of no object to me. Plus, I trust you, Jaime. You do good work, and I don't believe you to be someone that takes advantage." As Brent said this, Jaime let loose a small smile, and his eyes darted over to the cross for a split second, then back to Brent.

"So, is that all you needed to see me for, Brent and Patrick?" Jaime said, as he looked at both Brent and Patrick when he said their names.

", there is one more thing I wanted to ask you about, Jaime," Brent said, as he leaned in towards Jaime's desk. His heartbeat was racing now. Patrick also leaned in close, for he wanted to hear how this conversation would go.

"And what might that be?" Jaime said kind of confused at the current moment as to what Brent was going to ask him.

"Do you know anyone by the name of David Webb?"

Jaime looked calm as he answered the question with no faults or breaks in his speech.

"You mean the movie character David Webb? Like, Jason Bourne's identity, David Webb?" Jaime asked.

"No, I mean, like, a real person named David Webb," Brent said, sounding sort of agitated and annoyed.

"No, I can't say I have, sorry," Jaime answered calmly. He glanced over at the cross, looking at the starving Jesus.

"How about someone named Henry Boman?"

"No, I do not. Why do you want to know if I know these people, Brent?" Jaime was starting to sound less calm and maybe a little nervous. "Am I supposed to know them?" he whispered.

"Oh. Well, no. Maybe not. I'm asking because a little earlier today..." Brent glanced over at Patrick, seeing if he should tell Jaime what happened with Ken. Patrick nodded his head vertically. "We met up with Ken," Jaime looked as if he knew where this was going, "and he told us, not meaning to, that...well, we aren't who we think we are."

"Now what is that supposed to mean?" Jaime asked. He seemed to grow an interest in what Brent was saying.

"I mean, like, I'm not Brent McIlrath, and Patrick isn't Patrick Armstrong. He told us that we were lobotomized for some reason, he didn't tell us what, and said we were given new names and new lives. He also told us our old names were David Webb and Henry Boman." Jaime began to nod his head. "He said that we were given fake identities and fake memories that way we believed what we were given, so that way what Ken was doing wouldn't get to any sort of media. Ken also told us that Patrick and I were made rich and poor," At that, Jaime looked at Patrick and started noticing that maybe he was homeless. He just assumed that he chose to wear those clothes today and maybe stepped in some mud, or something. After all, Brent's clothes were dirty, too.

Brent continued, "This way we wouldn't meet with each other again, unlocking these memories of our real past. Plus," Brent leaned his head forward and pointed towards his flower-shaped scar on his forehead and said, "this mark is a lobotomy scar; Patrick has one that looks like this, too." Patrick showed his. Jaime's eyes widened at the sight.

"Also, Ken mentioned something about if anyone calls us 'Brent or Patrick' then they were in on what happened, and if they called us 'David or Henry' then they have no part in what happened. Now, we wanted to ask you if you had heard about any of this. Patrick and I were thinking of how we should take this information, and so far, we haven't come up with a solution."

Jaime took note of everything Brent had said to him, and Jaime glanced over at Patrick a few times and over at his cross while thinking about their situation. After a while, Jaime finally said something, "Have you met anyone yet who has called you either 'David or Henry'?"

Patrick finally said something. "No, we have not. The only person we've talked to after Ken is you."

"Well then," Jaime said, calmly, and sounding a little smug, "It sounds like you two got tricked by old Ken! I remember he was always a trickster, and it sounds like he still is. Listen; if I were in your position, I would just pay no mind to what Ken said, in fact just forget about him. If he's still pranking you, and to this extreme mind you, then you probably shouldn't be friends with him anymore. I'd say just don't talk to him ever again, make him feel like he won and you two went on a dumb journey just to look like fools at Ken's expense."

Patrick turned to Brent, "See? I told you that's what happened!" He turned back to Jaime, "Thank you for clearing this up for us, Jaime."

"No problem. Now, is there something else you want to ask me about?" Jaime locked his fingers once more and pulled up his chair so that he would look a little more professional.

"No..." Brent sounded defeated when he spoke. Brent and Patrick then stood up, along with Jaime, who shook their hands and showed them the door; politely might I add.

"Alright, you two take care now!" Jaime said, as Patrick started to open the door. As Brent was halfway through the door, he looked back. He saw Jaime adjusting things on his desk, especially the cross, which he was constantly moving to get it in the perfect position. He also noticed something that he hadn't seen at first when he walked in earlier. He walked back into the room.

"Hey, Jaime," he started, "What's that behind you, on that table?"

Jaime turned around in his chair to look at a table that was perpendicular to the glass wall. There laid a necklace, laced in rubies, sapphires and emeralds. Jaime picked up the necklace, and put it in its velvet container, which lie right next to the necklace. Jaime turned around, and showed the necklace to Brent.

"It's my anniversary present for Acacia. Our anniversary is next Friday; I bought the necklace today after I got done working in the field."

"Huh," Brent said, as he started to walk up to Jaime's desk. Patrick turned around to find Brent walking back into the room. *"What the hell, Brent..."* Patrick thought. After Patrick reentered the room with Brent, Brent continued to press

Jaime, "So how much do you make a year, Jaime? About $50,000, or so would you say?"

"That's none of your business! Why do you want to know?" Jaime started to get a little defensive.

"Because I want to know how you were able to afford that necklace." Brent said, as he looked at the dazzling necklace. It looked to reflect the light reflecting from the lights in the ceiling. It hurt Brent's eyes to look at it any longer, so he looked away from the necklace and focused his attention on Jaime. Every now and again he would glance at the necklace, to look at its beauty.

"Well," Jaime said, as he was calming his nerves, "you are right when you accuse this of being a pricy necklace," he pointed to the necklace, "and I'm affording it by taking out some loans from the bank, cutting some corners in our budget, you know, things like that. It will be paid off eventually. It's all worth it to see my Acacia smile, though."

"But you know, something about this seems too convenient," Brent said; he started to pace the room, "I say this because Ken, when he told us that, 'prank', he said that what he was a part of paid him good money."

"What is that supposed to mean?" Jaime said sounding a little angered by what Brent is imposing on him. Jaime then looked down at the necklace and then back up to Brent.

"What I'm saying is that I think you've been lying to us, too." Brent put his hands on the desk. "I think that you know what happened to us, and you're trying to hide it. You're like Ken, you don't want this incident to go public, and so you're trying to cover it up. How much of that is true, tell me?"

"Wha-None! Nothing that you said is true, and I'm hurt that that's what you think of me!" Jaime's eyes looked unwary as they darted from the necklace, to the cross, and to Brent; he sometimes looked at Patrick, but only for a few seconds.

"OK, how about another refresher. What about when we first walked into your office, huh? Remember what you said to us?"

Jaime, trying to recall, put his eyes in the right side of his eye sockets.

"I said, and I quote, 'Oh, well hello Brent! And why hello to you too, Patrick! I didn't expect to see you here!'" Jaime said. He looked to be proud of himself.

Brent started to get excited.

"Oh no. That's where you're wrong. When we walked in, the first thing you said was, 'Oh well hello Day-uh, Brent!' I think you tried stopping yourself from saying someone's name that started with a, 'Day' sound. Gee, the first thing that pops into my mind is the name, 'David', which, according to Ken, is my real name. Explain that one, Mr. Architect."

"Well, uh..." Jaime's eyes went into the left-hand corner of his eye sockets. "You're right; I did almost call you 'David'. That's because the person who was I here before you guys showed up, his name was David. My mind just put his name for yours. If that's what you are upset about, then I'm sorry about that. That what you want to hear, Brent?"

Brent started to get excited; Patrick looked to take note of everything that was happening.

"That's a lie." Jaime gulped. "Before walking into your office, I looked at the appointment sheet behind the secretary's desk. We walked into your business at 2:45, and a man by the name of George Butler was scheduled for today, November 22nd, at 2:30. No one else had an appointment for today, so that means the man who you had before us was George Butler, not a man named David!" Brent's speech started to go a little quick, but Patrick and Jaime could still make out what he was saying.

"Um...uh..." Jaime started to crack. Patrick, on the other hand, was also worried. Not because he was in the position Jaime was, but because he's afraid Brent might be right.

"Plus," Brent went on, "Ken said the same thing when he accidentally called Patrick, 'Henry'. He said that he worked with a person named Henry. You, though, said that your previous client was named David. Although, the thing you both agreed on was that your mind processed it wrong. So, process this in your mind; own up to it. Just tell us, 'Yes, he wasn't telling the truth, nor was I!' That's all I want to hear."

Jaime just about had it with Brent and his questions. He turned red, and exploded, "Is that what you want to hear, huh? You want me to tell you that your name is David Webb, a middle-class punk who didn't know when to stop; the man that was always too sympathetic for his own good? You also want me to tell Patrick here that he's Henry Boman, the guy who never thought his actions through? If that's what you want, then there you go! That's true; you were lobotomized, and I've regretted doing it ever since! There, are you satisfied now? Are you done pestering me with these fucking belligerent questions about NOTHING?!?" Jaime heaved heavily after he was done talking. He calmed down and looked at Brent and Patrick. Their faces were pale, and their palms were loose. Both couldn't believe what came out of Jaime's mouth, and worst of all, they learned that what Ken told them was true.

That was the most shocking thing to Brent and Patrick that day; seeing Jaime act like this.

Brent removed his hands from Jaime's desk, and he stumbled as he began to sit down in one of the two chairs in Jaime's office. Patrick joined Brent in sitting down, except he was a bit more collected than Brent was.

"Listen, I'm sorry about snapping at you two. I guess my anger got the best of me..." Brent and Patrick looked up at him, both glaring at Jaime. "...that's not what you two want to hear is it?" Brent and Patrick didn't reply. "Right, I get it. Yeah, I was a part of what happened to you two. But hear me out, please?" Brent and Patrick look at Jaime, wanting to hear what he had to say. Jaime glanced over at his cross before he started to speak again. "Listen, I never wanted to hurt you two. You two were good friends to me, and when I had to take part in the lobotomy, I felt horrible. Both in doing the action and the guilt that came along with it. No amount of words or, "Sorrys," can make up what I did to you two."

"Can you tell us what you were doing that made us have to be lobotomized?" Patrick asked him.

"I cannot; against policy." Jaime said.

"So, I guess that means you're like Ken, then?" Brent asked.

"No, I'm not like him. His entire life seems to revolve around *this*" he put heavy emphasis on 'this', "while I, after your lobotomies, haven't been the same man...I go to bed every night thinking about that day, and what I could have done differently."

"I assume you still work for them, then?"

"Yes, you assumed right, Brent. I still work for that company..."

"Can you give us the name of your company?" asked Patrick.

"No. That, too, is a secret I shall not say. I know it could bring you two some peace of mind, but I just can't do that. I'm sorry..." Jaime hung his head low and put his hands behind his head.

"So why do you still work for this company and/or group?" Brent asked Jaime, trying to maybe get something out of him.

"Like I've said, I hated doing that to you guys. In fact, I hate doing what I'm doing for that company. Granted all I do for it is write up the reports and results..." he stopped himself before giving away any further information. "Anyway, to answer your question, the only reason I'm still working for that company is because the pay is extraordinary. Not that I care about the money, per say, but I still do it for Acacia. I want her to have the best, and now with a baby coming, I feel like I have to keep working for this company." Jaime sighed.

Brent asked Jaime, "Does Acacia know about this company, what happened to us, what you do for it?"

"Acacia? Oh, no. She's kind of an airhead, to be honest. She thinks that this architecture thing racks in all the money I provide for her. I love the woman, but she's about as smart as a box of rocks sometimes..." He paused, then continued on to say, "From this company I work for, I've been able to pay for so many things. It helped Acacia and I have a good wedding, an amazing reception, and a relaxing honeymoon. I was thinking of quitting this company, cutting my losses, and working on what this architecture job could give me. I was going to try and better myself, but..."

"...then the baby happened, right?" Brent said, finishing Jaime's sentence.

"Yes...and I can't just quit now. I have a family to support, and Acacia doesn't work. I want my baby to have the best, just like I do with Acacia." Jaime slammed his head down onto his desk. His voice was muffled. "Like I said, I'm sorry about what happened to you two. I want to quit, I really do, believe me, but it's just..." Jaime lifted his head a little from the desk and buried his hands in his head. "I just...I don't know..." he then sat there for an elongated period. Brent and Patrick said nothing, hoping that Jaime would revitalize himself and say something else, but nothing came out from him. Patrick sort of felt bad for Jaime, in a way; Brent's feelings were mutual.

Eventually Brent said, "Jaime, we understand how you must feel. I feel the same way about my situation, and I assume Patrick is with his. We don't know whether we want to keep finding out these things about ourselves." Brent looked over at Patrick for support. He nodded and Patrick continued Brent's speech.

"Yeah, I feel the same way about this, Brent. And Jaime, we aren't going to get all up in your grill about this either. We just want answers; that's all. We aren't going to beat you down to a pulp if you don't comply!" Patrick said, with a little bit of sarcasm in his voice.

Jaime just answered back, with his head still being cradled by his hands, "I just...I don't know anymore..."

Brent walked over to him, put his arm on his shoulder and said softly, "You say you're sorry, so prove it to us. You want to make yourself a better man; this is how you do it. We want answers, so we'll give you a day to recoup, and then we'll come back for some answers tomorrow, OK?"

Jaime didn't reply. He just laid there motionless, as if he was just hoping this nightmare he's been living would end already.

With this, Brent and Patrick decided to walk out of Jaime's room for good this time. They got up and opened the door. Brent looked back at Jaime, to see his head still enveloped by his hands, and the necklace in its velvet casing lying next to Jaime; the cross seemed to reflect some sort of light onto Jaime's head. Jaime said to himself, not knowing that Brent was still present, "I just…I don't know anymore…"

Chapter 11

-Heart is a Hole; Cherri Bomb-

Reentering the outside world from Jaime's business, the two men realized the town was now enveloped in a dark twilight, almost pitch black.

"Wow, it sure is dark..." Patrick said as they walked out of the door from Jaime's Wood.

"Yeah, it sure is..." Brent was checking the time on his phone. "6:00PM" it read. "It's 6:00? Wow...I guess we were in there for a while?"

"Must be...it only felt like a few minutes..." Patrick said, as he looked up at the beautiful sky that was displayed above them.

"OK, so do you want to head back with me to Ken's shop? I need to pick up my limo from there," Brent asked Patrick. He was already starting to walk back to the shop.

"Well," Patrick said, as he caught up with Brent, "I don't really want to be reminded of that asshole, but I guess I'll tag along."

A few moments of silence existed while the two awkwardly walked towards the shop, not really knowing what to say to each other.

"Hey, uh," Patrick said, scratching the back of his head while saying so, "I want to...um...apologize."

"Hmm?" Brent looked over with a puzzled look on his face.

"I doubted you, and it's obvious I shouldn't have. So, I'm sorry about that."

"It's OK. I'm a little glad you did doubt me. You put me back in my place a bit."

Patrick looked a little confused by this, but smiled said back, "Yeah, I guess...but I don't know. When we were back there talking with Jesse, you were so fired up about this whole subject...I've never seen you like that before. I kinda like this new version of Brent. Keep with it!" Brent laughed at this, and after that, the two men walked back to the shop, not uttering a single word to each other until they reached their destination; they were trying to reconstruct the mental damage that had been done to their minds as the day progressed. Brent and Patrick also were thinking about what they wanted to do, let alone think about, with Jaime's information that he told them.

While walking back to "Heavy Metal", the two continuously looked up into the night sky. It was a hue of orange, since it was still twilight, but the black of the darkness was starting to overcome the orange. The orange tried valiantly to stay alive, but eventually the darkness of night would overcome the orange. The display of colors battling to stay alive made the two men content with what they went through this day. It was a beautiful sight that both Brent and Patrick wanted to enjoy every second of.

When Brent and Patrick arrived at "Heavy Metal" it was already nighttime. The two men's only sources of navigation were the streetlights that lit their way. Patrick opened the door to Ken's shop, and he entered the lobby with Brent following swiftly behind. Brent looked over and saw Pam; their eyes met and Pam's face went white and she quickly looked away. Brent scanned the room a little more and saw S sitting in one of the chairs with his head low, and his eyes staring at the floor.

"Hello, S," said Brent, as he walked over towards him.

S looked up and his eyes met Brent's. "Hello, Brent." He looked relieved to see him. God only knows how long he was sitting there, just doing nothing. He looked behind Brent and saw Patrick standing there. "Who's…uh…?"

"Oh, yes. Sorry, almost forgot something important. S, this here is Patrick. Patrick, this is S." Brent introduced the two, and Patrick and S shook each other's hands.

"Hello, sir; pleasure to meet you." Patrick said to S, as he shook his hand.

"Aye, and to you too," S replied. The two stopped shaking hands.

"S, Patrick is a very close friend of mine from High School. He's homeless, and I'm making accommodations for him to stay at the mansion, even if it is only for one night. Are you OK with this, S?" Brent asked S.

"I don't think that's my call, Mr. McIlrath," S began to say, "If you want your friend to stay at the mansion, then he will be welcomed by all the staff until he departs, and then some." S smiled at Patrick as he finished his statement.

"Well, uh, thank you...S," Patrick retorted. He seemed a little on edge from the way S treated him; he's not used to such kindness.

"So, um, S," Brent changed the subject, "Is the limo done being worked on?

"Why yes it has. In fact, it's been done for about, oh, 10 minutes or so. I was going to call you, but I got lost deep into my thoughts..." S started to drift away, "Anyhow, if you want to we can just go back into the workshop and pick up your car; we can be out of here in mere moments then."

Patrick didn't like the idea of seeing Ken again, and Brent thought the same thing. But Brent decided that they had to man up sometime; why not now?

"Yeah, sure! Patrick, S, follow me." Brent then lead the two back into the workshop that Ken resided in. Brent decided that he was going to play dumb to Ken, and act as if what happened earlier never happened. He hoped that Patrick would follow his façade, and maybe Ken would too, though he doubted it. As Brent opened the door into the workshop, he noticed the car Ken was working on earlier was no longer in the shop, and it was replaced with Brent's limo. The foldable chairs that were also there were gone, too. The blood that used to be there had disappeared as well. It looked to be an entirely new scene.

Ken heard the noise of the door and spun around to see who it was.

"Hello there, Brent. Patrick. S," Ken greeted the three men with a slur in his speech. His face was still tender looking, and purple, too. Some spots on his face had dried blood and cuts, along with bandages. His mouth still looked wreck from earlier as well.

"Hello again, Ken," said Brent, as he was the only one to even speak to Ken during this time.

"So, I assume you're here to see about your car, eh?" he said, sounding like he was speaking with water in his mouth.

"You guessed right." Brent was being awfully happy with Ken. Brent looked upon his black colored limo; it seemed to deem forth a new shiny look.

"Well, you're all set to go! I've been done for a while now; I've just been sitting here, adding a few things to your car. I put a little wax on the limo, just because, you know..." He looked at Brent with sorrowful eyes.

"Yeah, well thank you, Ken! I appreciate it," Brent said back. He walked up to the limo and slid his hand over the hood of the limo. It was slick as slick could be; Brent wanted to slide his hand over the wax-covered car, but instead he stopped himself from doing so.

"So, what was wrong with the car?" Brent asked Ken, as Brent turned around from the car and looked at Ken.

"Well, the limo's problem was that the engine overheated, which is odd considering that it's cold as ice outside. Nevertheless, I cooled down the engine, which wasn't very hard to do, and replaced the thermostat. I also realized that your tires needed rotated, too. So, decided to throw that in there; free of charge. In fact, you don't even need to pay me for the work; it's my treat."

"Really? Wow, thanks Ken!" Brent created fake enthusiasm, though he was really a little happy on the inside.

"Yeah, well I figured that's what friends do, right?"

"Right..." Brent looked uncomfortable now. He didn't make eye contact with Ken, either. "Well...are we good to go then?"

"Yep. She's all yours."

"Alright, cool," Brent said, as he now changed his attention from Ken towards S. "You got the keys?" S pulled out the keys from his jacket pocket and twirled them around his index finger. "Alright then," Brent said, clapping his hands together, "Let's get rolling!" S walked up to the limo and unlocked all the doors to the limo. S opened the back-compartment's door, and quickly shoved Brent and Patrick into it; he was secretly very cold, and wanted to get out of this workshop as fast as he could. S closed the door as Patrick got his foot free of the door. As S got into the driver's seat, Ken raised the garage door so that the limo could depart from the workshop.

"You ever been in a limo before?" Brent asked Patrick as they both started to get comfortable in the seats of the back compartment of the limo.

"Nope," replied Patrick.

"Well you are now," Brent said. As the words escaped his mouth, the limo's engine started up again, and S peeled out of the workshop and into the streets of Preston, Oklahoma.

The headlights of the limo cut through the darkness that nightfall bestowed upon the town. Brent leaned forward and opened the glass pane so that he could speak to S.

"Hey, S," Brent started, "would you mind if you drove us to 'Music Nightly', the bar? Hang on," Brent cocked his head back to speak to Patrick. "Hey, Patrick, want to go to a bar?"

"Sure!" Patrick replied. He was still relaxing in the comfort that the limo's seats brought to him.

"Yeah, can you drive us to 'Music Nightly', S?" Brent said, as he turned his back to the direction of S.

"You're the boss, Brent," S said, as he turned on his left turn signal and turned left. Brent then slid the glass pane closed again, and sunk back into his seat.

"So, what do you think of the limo, Patrick?" Brent asked.

"It's awesome!" Patrick replied, "It's so...comfortable."

"You think that's the best part? Well watch this..." Brent pulled out his phone and plugged it into the jack that played music through the speakers in the back compartment of the limo. He turned on his phone, and noticed that it was now 6:20PM, and that his battery only had a 40% charge left in it. He paid no mind to it as he went to his music app and put his playlist of shuffle. Brent and Patrick rocked out to music all the way down to the bar.

After a few minutes, the limo started to slow down, and eventually came to a stop. Brent turned off the music on his phone, and took out the jack from the input jack. He slid open the glass pane and asked S, "I guess we're here, then?"

"Yep," replied S, "You're free to get out at any time you like."

"Alright cool. Hey, S, you want to come in with us? It'll be my treat."

"No, but thank you, Brent. The wife wouldn't like it if she found out I went to a bar. She's probably already going to have a fit that I'm going to be home late tonight..."

"OK, well then you can go ahead and drive back to the mansion and leave."

"You sure about me leaving, boss?"

"Yeah, it's fine with me." Brent began fixing his jacket, and realized how dirty it looked. He figured that he's not going to the bar to pick up girls, so who really cares.

"But, sir, how are you going to get home?" asked S.

"Like a normal person; I'll take a cab."

"Well, I guess that would be sensible..." S said in his slow voice.

"I'll be fine, don't worry about me." Brent stopped fiddling with his suit and began to look at S again. "Enjoy a nice glass of wine with the wife, S!"

"If you say so, sir." S said. It wasn't hard to tell that he was eager to get home. Brent slid the glass pane to the closed position again, and he turned around in the limo to see Patrick in the back, with his excitement exploding.

"You ready?" Brent asked Patrick.

"Whenever you are," Patrick retorted, as Brent then opened the right-hand side door; it swung open graciously.

Brent was greeted to bright neon lights that were hung above the entrance to the bar. It read, "Music Nightly." Brent moved away from the car door, and Patrick soon got out as well. As Patrick departed from the limo, Brent shut the door and walked up to the passenger seat's window and gave it a thumbs up. S saw that thumbs up from inside the car, and then he drove away, leaving Brent and Patrick there to enjoy their night at the bar.

After watching S drive away with the limo, Brent and Patrick turned their attention towards the bar once more and began walking towards the door. When at the door, the two noticed a flyer on the door which read, "DISTORTED TIME – TONIGHT'S ENTERTAINMENT – 7:00PM"

"Distorted Time?" Brent thought out loud, "That name sounds familiar."

"Yeah, it does to me too," Patrick added, "Maybe it's has something to do with our pasts?"

"Maybe…" Brent thought about it for a few seconds, and then decided he didn't want to think about it too hard. "Let's not worry about all that right now, let's go ahead and get a drink, shall we? Take a load off?" Brent then opened the door and allowed Patrick to enter the bar ahead of him.

Brent and Patrick walked into the bar, and the force of the door closing almost swept Brent and Patrick off their feet. The inside of the bar was basic, as there was a bar to their left, and a few tables to their right, with some people inhabiting them. Towards the back of the room lay a few more tables, with no one in them, and what looked to be a stage. There were amps and a drum set lined up on the stage, and a person walking around the equipment plugging in things, unplugging things, turning dials and what have you. Neither Brent nor Patrick knew how to properly set up amps, so they paid little to no attention to the man. Instead, Brent walked over towards the bar and took a seat, with Patrick following closely behind in Brent's footsteps. The bar stools were empty, except for a suspicious looking man at the end of the bar. He wore a long brown overcoat, and his hair was messed. A hat sat next to him, as he sipped on a drink. Every sip was long and very drawn out; it was as if he was waiting for something, or someone. Due to the mystery that this man seemed to give off, Brent and Patrick slid down a few seats to get farther away from this man. Patrick sat closer to the man, as he was sitting to the right of Brent.

The bartender walked over to Brent and Patrick and asked, "Good evening, gentlemen. Can I get you something?"

"Uh, yeah…" Brent paused and thought of what he wanted, but Patrick was quick to the trigger.

"I'll have a Budweiser," Patrick said to the bartender.

"I'll have what he's having as well." Brent pointed to Patrick as he said this. The bartender then turned around and started to fix the drinks.

Not but seconds later the bartender turned around with two opened Budweiser bottles. "Enjoy," said the bartender as he laid down the drinks in front of Brent and Patrick. He walked away from the two men, and tended to the creepy man at the end of the bar's needs.

Brent took a drink of his beer, and turned to face Patrick. Patrick seemed as if he's never had a beer before, as his mouth scrunched up after taking a drink.

"It's been a while since you've had a taste of that, huh?" Brent asked him.

"Yeah...you could say that." Patrick replied.

"OK, so I know I said let's not think about our pasts tonight, but it's eating at me," Brent said as he took another sip of his drink.

"Same here..." Patrick sorrowfully said as he, too, drank from his bottle.

Brent put down his drink and said towards Patrick, "So after what just happened with Jaime, do you believe now that we were lobotomized?"

"I don't like to admit it," Patrick took off his green beanie and laid it down onto the bar. His hair looked like a mop; wet and dirty. However, it was acceptable seeing as he probably hasn't had a shower in a while. He ran his hand through his long hair as he replied, "And I am still a bit skeptical, but I believe what both Ken and Jaime told us might be true."

"So, what do you suggest we do now?" asked Brent. "I mean, we can go back to Jaime tomorrow and hope to get something out of him?" He took another drink of his beer.

"I don't know." Patrick took a huge gulp of his drink. He choked a little bit, but he soon got over it. He took a few more drinks of his beer, and then finally thought of a reply to Brent's question. "I guess we can go back and see Jaime again tomorrow; see if we can't get more information out of him. But...I am still a little held back about all this."

"How do you mean?"

"It all just seems too surreal to me. We met up today, and then we find out it just so happens that we used to have some huge history together that neither of us knew about?" Patrick said truthfully. Brent looked away as Patrick continued, "Maybe Jaime was in with Ken on this 'prank' thing? We can't just rule that possibility out."

"While true, that's always a possibility we must keep in mind, I don't think that's the case. Jaime seemed distraught when talking about us and our lobotomies; I don't think he's that good of an actor to play up to something like this. I believe his pain was real, and that our lobotomies were real, too."

Patrick looked down and at his bottle for a few seconds. He looked up and said, "Yeah, that makes sense, too...there's just too many unknown variables in everything we learned today; it's hard to make the right choice, or even a choice that seems logical."

"I know, but just trust me on this, Patrick. With what Jaime told us a little bit ago, I'm more convinced than earlier that there's something more to this. And I want to find out what it is. So, are you going to help me with this, or not?"

"Well with a speech like that how can I say no?" Patrick smugly said, smirking while speaking. The two then clinked their bottles together and took a drink in unison.

"Hello everyone in Music Nightly! How you all doing' to-night?" A voice came from the direction that seemed to be the stage. The voice that rang throughout the bar seemed to be amplified. Brent, Patrick, the people who sat at the tables and even the creepy man at the end of the bar turned around to see who was speaking. On the stage, there was a hipster-looking white male who was wearing glasses and a Polo shirt. He wore tore up jeans and a leather belt as well. The entity of counterculture continued on to say, "Alright, we have a new band to see this stage tonight! So please give them a warm welcome; I introduce to you, Distorted Time!"

The people in the bar clapped as the band took the stage. Brent pulled out his phone and checked the time.

"6:50PM" it read. He whispered into Patrick's ear, "They're 10 minutes early…"

Patrick whispered back, "Oh, who cares?"

When all the band was on the stage, and they had their instruments ready to go, the lead singer walked up to the microphone. The band consisted of two women and three men; two of the men were white, while one of them was black. The lead singer looked to be about 28, or so, he was African American and was very scrawny. His hair was nonexistent, as his head was bald, and he wore a sweatband on his wrist. He sported a white undershirt, which had a black jacket over top of the shirt, a yellow tie, black jeans, and black and white colored sneakers.

The "crowd" was still clapping as the singer walked up to the microphone. "Thank you, thank you," said the man, as the clapping quieted down. "Good evening ladies and gentlemen. As you've just heard, we are Distorted Time, and we want to start off our show with a little something to get everyone in the mood for some rock music! Now, I have a story that I want to tell you all; it's of one man's slow decline, and when a girl yanked on the strings to break this man's heart." The man stepped away from the microphone as one of the girls, the lead guitarist, started slamming away on her guitar, creating some nasty licks. Soon after she started, the other girl, the bassist, and one of the other guys, the other guitarist, started to add onto the beat that the lead guitarist had started. Once the three stopped playing their section of the song, the drummer then joined in as all the members of the band started to play their song in time with the beat.

Throughout the show, you could tell that this might have been the band's first ever show, but they seemed to be having fun, and that's all that really mattered. They didn't sound too bad, either. Everyone in the bar started to tap their feet, fingers, or whatever else to the beats that the band was creating. Well, everyone except the creepy guy at the end of the bar; he just kept considering his glass at his drink, and looked up every occasionally, to look at the door. Brent and Patrick, however, enjoyed themselves to the free entertainment and even found themselves humming some of the songs even after the show was over. Brent and Patrick liked what they heard, and soon those tunes that they were humming and tapping to the beat of would have a much closer spot to them then they would have imagined.

Chapter 12

-Goodnight, Fair Lady; Coheed and Cambria-

Once the band had played their last song for the night, the lead vocalist said into the microphone, "Thank you everyone for being such an awesome crowd! And thank you to Music Nightly for making that show possible! We'll be hanging around the bar for a little while, so go ahead and talk to us, if you want!" The band then put their instruments where they originally were and walked off the stage.

"Wow!" Brent shouted, as he turned to face Patrick, "That was awesome!"

"I know. My ears are still ringing; I forgot how loud these concerts were," Patrick shouted.

"I mean, those guitar riffs were catchy," Brent said loudly.

"Yeah, and the bass helped add that groove to the songs," Patrick said, a little less loud this time. The two's hearing started to come back; the ringing began to dim.

"The drums were also very well implemented into the songs. They really helped create the beat of the song."

"Indeed. I think what I might have liked most was the vocals, to be honest," Patrick said.

"I was about to say the same thing," Brent said quickly. "I thought the vocals were very clear, and from what I could tell the lyrics had some form of meaning to them; you could see the lead vocalist having fun up on the stage. Then again, all of the members of the band looked as if they were having fun."

"Yeah, all of the band members seemed to be having a good time. That's what I liked a lot about this band; they looked as if they were having fun. And more power to them; I know I sure as hell can't sing, better yet play an instrument." Patrick drank the last gulp of his beer and put the bottle down aside from where he could immediately grab it.

It was at this point in which a man, whom had just sat down by Patrick not but a few moments ago, turned to face the two men and started to talk to them.

"Excuse me, sorry to interrupt, but I overheard you two talking and I was wondering; would you two happen to be David Webb and Henry Boman?"

Brent and Patrick were shocked about this man's words, especially the last segment. Brent was already looking at the man, but Patrick had to swivel around to see who the man speaking to them was. To their surprise, it was the lead singer from the band they just watched, Distorted Time.

Patrick looked at Brent, as they exchanged reactions and expressions. Brent looked at Patrick with doubt. "Um…" started Brent, looking still at Patrick, hoping he could supply some form of direction for Brent to take. Patrick just did a slight nod and Brent continued, hoping that was his right of way, "Yes, yes I am David, and he's," Brent pointed to Patrick, "Henry Boman. Who-Who's asking?"

The singer looked puzzled. "Really, you don't remember me? Well that just rustles my jimmies! Whatever, I guess…" The man rubbed his head, "I'll just say my name then; Hey guys! It's me, Remi Chandler!"

"Remi?" Brent and Patrick both exclaimed. Memories started to rush into their minds, as both started to recall who this "Remi" guy is. Brent was the first to talk, "Holy crap, I remember you! Yeah, we went to High School together; we were friends!"

"That we were," said Remi.

"Wow, how long were you sitting there, Remi?" Patrick said, as he turned back around to see Remi again.

"Eh, long enough I'd say." Remi smiled.

"Sorry about not noticing you at first," Brent expressed, "You just look so different than you did back in High School."

"Nah, it's cool. I only noticed you two because your voices sound almost the same, with a little variation. Plus, you both don't look so different either. Well, maybe a little dirtier…" Remi said this as he looked at Brent and Patrick's clothing, which wasn't the cleanest material ever.

"Yeah, sorry about that," Brent said, "It's been quite a long day."

"I hear ya," Remi stated. He turned and motioned to the bartender. "Get me a Bud Light, por favor."

"You got it, sir." The bartender then turned around, grabbed a bottle and opened it for Remi. He gave him the bottle and said, "Don't worry; this one's on me, sir. You guys did a hell of a job up on stage."

"Why, thank you!" Remi replied with a huge smile on his face.

As this was going on, Brent looked past Patrick and Remi and looked at the creepy man at the end of the bar. He had a new drink, which was just about full. Just then, the door to the right of Brent swung open, and a pretty young girl walked in, with long black hair, pale white skin, and a grey shirt with jeans on. She walked up to the bar quick and got herself a drink. The bartender gave her the drink, and she walked off to a nearby table and sat down; alone. The creepy man was looking upon her, trying not to seem like he was staring at her.

All the while, Patrick and Remi kept talking. Patrick started off by saying, "So, Remi, congrats on this whole band thing!"

"Thank you, Henry," Remi said back. Patrick still wasn't content with the whole, "Henry Boman", thing yet.

"Weren't you in a band ever since, what was it, sophomore year in High School?"

"You got that right. Funny you should ask, because my band, Distorted Time, actually has gone through a few member changes throughout the past 11 years, or so."

"Wow. You've been in a band for 11 years? It's hard to imagine that I know someone who's in a band, let alone in one for so long."

"Well thank you," Remi said. He looked down at the floor, and then back up at Patrick again. "Anyway, as I was saying, our guitarist and bassist for the band has changed about," Remi paused and thought for a second, "I think it's three times now? I don't know; in any case, our band now, I think, is solid.

While Remi and Patrick were talking about the band, Brent was still fixated on the story of the creepy man. Overtime, he eventually got up, put on his hat, and carried his drink, as well as himself, over to the table in which the girl was sitting at. It looked as if he asked if he could sit with her; she agreed, as the man then sat down in an open chair at her table. He looked to be trying to charm her, as she kept blushing and giggling at some of the things this man was saying to her. This went on for a while, so Brent turned his attention away from the antics of the creepy man and again listened to Remi.

"So..." Brent began to ask Remi, "How's life been going?"

"Good, I guess. I don't mean to tell you my life story, but three weeks ago I broke up with my girlfriend of eight months."

"Oh, well I'm sorry to hear that." Brent said, sympathizing with Remi.

"Yeah, we'll that's life, you know," Remi said seeming kind of down about the situation.

"What was her name, if you don't mine me asking," Patrick asked as he joined in on the conversation.

"Her name was Diane Cummings, and she was a beauty to say the least." Remi looked down at the floor again and started to chuckle. "You know, there was this really funny moment we shared, and I will always keep that moment close to me." Brent leaned in closer to Remi, and Patrick turned to where his right ear was closer to Remi's voice. The way Patrick was facing gave him a perfect view of the creepy man and his attempts to pick up that pretty lady. From what he could tell, it looked as if the man was trying to be kind, maybe even polite to the lady. Patrick couldn't hear the two, of course, but their facial expressions and reactions were enough to help deduce Patrick's accusation.

During the time in which Patrick was fixated on the man's feeble attempt at love, Remi began with his story; Patrick, while facing the creepy man and poor woman, was no longer paying attention to them. He spaced out and was now only really paying attention to the story Remi was telling the

two   men.
    "Once during the time what Diane and I dated, I had to go up to St. Louis, Missouri for something; I don't recall exactly what it was for. Anyway, I asked Diane if she wanted to go with me. She agreed and said she always wanted to go see The Arch, eat at a few places, etc. So, we drove there, because flying is too mainstream," he said this sarcastically, "And when we arrived I immediately did what I needed to there and we enjoyed the rest of that night and the next day in STL; we booked a hotel prior to leaving. So, the night of the first day we walked through the streets of St. Louis and eventually we found The Arch. It was gorgeous at night; lights reflecting off the surface, the feeling the cool late summer air provided...it was magical. Truly magical..." Remi paused and looked around for a moment or two, collecting his thoughts.
    "But I digress. So, anyway, we stood under The Arch, looking at it from up under, I left out a detail. It was a windy night in STL that night; that background info helps build up the joke. Regardless, we were standing under The Arch and Diane said, 'Oh my God! The Arch is swaying!' She's never been to a city where a building could sway. I say back to her, 'Yeah, buildings like this sway.' She then says back, and this is the funny part, 'Ooh, I'm scared! Please, Remi, can we go? I'm hecky scared!'
    Brent and Patrick just about exploded at this. It wasn't the fact that the buildup and then the payoff was funny, it was more of that what Diane supposedly said that was funny to them.
    Through broken laughs and gasps, Brent managed to say, "What...what the hell? What the hell is hecky scared?"
    "I don't know, I honestly don't know!" Remi said back, trying to hold back laughter. The three men continued to chuckle and giggle like school girls until they eventually settled down and grew silent.
    Remi broke the silence saying, "Yeah, Diane's a comedian, she does standup comedy at some no-name places around town here, and I used to show up to some of her shows...to be honest, I showed up to one of her shows a few days ago." Remi looked at the tables in the bar to his left;

he noticed a person shrouded behind a newspaper, a magazine, or something of the sort. He seemed to put down the paper he was looking at every occasionally, and look at the creepy man and the woman. Remi thought nothing of it and continued his story:

"Anyway, she uses that "hecky scared" excerpt in some of her shows...It gets better every time I tell the event so someone or I hear her retell the story." Remi looked at the bar, which his arm was now resting on. He sighed deeply. "God, I miss her..."

"Well, maybe you should go up and talk to her," Patrick said, as he too put his arm on the bar. Brent then followed, not wanting to feel left out. Patrick continued, "I don't remember, did you say that you left her or did she leave you?"

"I left her!" Remi said very quickly and before Patrick even finished his question.

Patrick doubted Remi as Patrick studied him for a few seconds, then said, "You're lying; I think you've been saying to people for the past few weeks, but I say that she left you, Remi."

Remi looked down and at his yellow tie. He sighed, "You got me, Henry. You done figured me out!" He laughed a little, "I don't like to think about it, but, yes, she dumped me. She told me that I needed to 'grow up' and stop spending so much time in my band; she said she thought it wasn't going to go anywhere. Well, I showed her! Tonight, was our first gig, and I think the rest will come to us in due time," He paused, "And that's mainly the reason as to why we broke up, was because of my band. She, at the time, was a comedian who had a steady work, every Friday night at the HaHa Club, 7PM; occasionally, she'd get a few more shows during the other days, but mainly she worked off that. I, on the other hand, still hadn't got a gig for the band, and so she said to us that we weren't going to go anywhere, and then she left me."

"Listen, Remi," said Brent. Remi looked up to meet Brent's eyes, "Just go up and talk to her tomorrow night at the HaHa Club after her show is over. Tell her that your band got their first gig, and the venue seemed to really like you guys, as well as the attendants. If you like her so much, don't be afraid of what might happen; cause if you don't do it then you'll never know what could have happened."

Remi started to tear up a bit. He sniffled and wiped his eyes. "Gee, that was beautiful, David. You know what? I think I'll take your and Henry's advice and go talk to her tomorrow; tell her what I really feel. Who knows, maybe I'll get lucky and we start going out again."

"That's the spirit, Remi!" said Patrick excitedly. Patrick then turned around involuntarily to face the creepy man and the woman again. Now the woman was putting on lipstick diligently, and trying to hide it from the man. The creepy man then reached across the table at the woman for some reason, Patrick couldn't depict what, and in doing so accidentally turned over the lady's glass, releasing the liquid which was contained in there for so little time. The man looked to be apologizing, and then got up from his seat and then walked up towards the bar.

During the time in which these events were transpiring, Brent and Remi were both silent, with the sound of people talking and the faint music being played over the speakers filling their ears. "Mind if we change the subject, David?" asked Remi.

"Sure, go ahead. What shall the topic be?" Brent adjusted his position in his chair to where he would be more comfortable.

"I wanted to ask," began Remi, "What have you two been doing since we last saw each other in High School?"

Patrick swiveled around to watch the creepy man approach the bar, but was then confronted by the question that Remi just threw at him. Patrick answered, "Actually, my memory is a bit foggy of the past few years, to be quite honest..." Patrick managed to keep a good conscience since, while sort of lying, he was telling a partial truth.

"Yeah, same applies to me; I don't really recall the past few years so well. Nothing really important happened, I guess," Brent said as he rubbed the lobotomy scar on his forehead. Every time he touched the mark it sent cold chills down his spine and all throughout his body. It was a good reminder as to what transpired with Ken, Jaime, and the supposed incident seven years ago.

"Aye, well you know what I've been up to the past few years," Remi started, "You know, being in a band and all. Hey, I remember when we were younger and it was you," He pointed towards Brent, "You," he pointed towards Patrick, "and Kevin who showed up to the band's garage practices occasionally. Man, those were some fun times…"

"That explain why I knew some of this band's beats, I guess," thought Brent. He said to Remi, "How is Kevin, do you know? I haven't seen him in such a long time."

While Brent and Remi continued their discussion about Kevin, Patrick was more paying attention towards the creepy man. From his previous mishap with spilling the drink, the man walked up towards the bar and the bartender walked over to him, and then walked away, fixing up a drink. The bartender returned, gave the man the drink, and then walked away again. The creepy man picked up the girl's drink and, while turning around to walk back to the girl's table, Patrick seemed to notice that the man's available hand seemed to glide atop the glass, and he did something with his fingers that looked to be on the rim of the glass. The creepy man then finished his 180 spin and started walking back towards the girl, who was patiently waiting for the man's return. The man got to the table, and gave the girl her drink, and moved his hand in the air, as if he was saying at the time, "I'm sorry again about what happened."

While these events were happening, Remi and Brent were completely oblivious to the actions of this man and continued to talk about Kevin.

Remi began, "Kevin has actually been doing pretty good. He's an astronomy teacher over at Preston High School, you know, our old high school. I guess he just couldn't bear the thought of leaving the good times behind, huh?" He snickered at his own joke.

"I guess so," Brent said; he adjusted his position in his chair again, "I remember him always having an interest in astronomy way back when, but I didn't really think he would actually being doing something astronomy related."

"Well why not?" Remi asked.

"I just thought that he would go into another profession, that's all. A teacher...well he just never seemed the type to be honest." Brent said this trying not to offend Remi; he assumed that Kevin and Remi were still good friends, seeing how Remi spoke of him.

"I guess I see where you are coming from...I don't know. I just know that whenever I got the call from him saying that he was going to be an astronomy teacher, I don't know, it just seemed to fit him, to me. It's hard to explain..." Remi looked away and rubbed his hands together.

"Hm." Brent agreed with what Remi was saying, but he didn't say it, per say. "Well it's been a while since I've seen Kevin...hey Remi." Remi looked up and gave Brent his undivided attention, "What time can I go visit Kevin at school tomorrow, do you know?"

"Well, school gets out at about 2:25PM, so I would assume that you could probably catch him alone at about 2:30. He tends to stick around after school is over for a while so he can grade papers, organize the next day's assignments, etcetera."

"Alright, cool,' Brent said, straightening up his back (he was hunched over for a few minutes and just now realized it), "I'll go see him tomorrow. I'll check and see if Henry wants to go with me, but he seems to be 'out of it' for the current moment..." Brent and Remi finally realized Patrick not paying attention to their conversation. Brent followed the direction in which Patrick was looking and he, too, saw the creepy man praying on a girl. Remi, not wanting to be left out on the fun, also looked at the man and woman.

The girl sitting with the man raised her glass to her lips and tipped the glass up into the air to where the liquid would flow down the inside of the glass and into her mouth. Just as she was about to swallow the drink, the man that Remi noticed looking at a newspaper sprung up out of seat and threw the newspaper down on the floor. He then pulled a gun from his overcoat that he was wearing.

"Halt!" the mysterious man yelled; Brent, Patrick, Remi, and everyone else in the bar was still out of fright, terror, and shock. The mysterious man then continued to yell, "Police!" he pulled out his badge from the same pocket as the gun was being cradled in. The officer walked up towards the creepy man and shoved him onto the table; the girl dropped drink, and let loose the liquids that were in her mouth. They were spit on the back of the creepy man, and a little bit of the drink was then splattered on the officer's hands. The glass hit the floor and shattered, and a few glass shards dug into the lady's jeans. Her skin, however, was undamaged to the residue. The officer then grabbed the creepy man's arm and locked them together with one of the officer's fists. He then put away his gun and began digging for his hand cuffs. Whilst doing so, he said to the man, "You are being arrested for possession of controlled substance." He pulled out the cuffs after digging around in his coat pocket for a bit and then proceeded to put the creepy man's hands into the cuffs. All the while, the creepy man was struggling to get loose and kept his eyes on the lady that was still sitting in her seat, stunned as to what she was witnessing. "You have the right to remain silent and to refuse to answer questions. Do you understand?" the officer began to say.

Brent, Patrick, and Remi saw the creepy man move his lips to what the officer was telling him, however they could not make out what he was trying to say. "Anything you do say may be used against you in a court of law. Do you understand?" said the officer, very loudly. The creepy man moved his lips once more. The officer went through all the Miranda Rights, all with the man moving his lips for one-word responses. Finally, the officer reached the final right, "Knowing and understanding your rights as I have explained them to you, are you willing to answer my questions without an attorney present?" The creepy man moved his lips for the final time, and as lips closed the officer grabbed the man and raised his body from the table and started to walk him towards the door. Brent, Patrick, and Remi looked away when the creepy man and the officer as they passed by them, for they didn't want to make eye contact with either of the men.

When the door closed after the police officer and the cuffed man walked through it, Brent, Patrick, and Remi all sat in their bar stools for a few moments, shocked as to what they saw go down just a few moments ago. Brent managed to shake his frozen state for a second or two and looked over at the woman, who was still sitting in her seat at her table, hands trembling and eyes watering. Her skin was pale as a ghost, and the bartender walked over to her to try and calm her down. Patrick then awoke from his state and shook Remi's shoulder; Remi then was taken out of his shocked state and was entered back into reality.

"You want to...go now?" Brent asked Patrick and Remi.

"Let's," said Remi and Patrick in unison.

Brent, Patrick and Remi then walked out of the bar, but before Brent left he pulled out a $20 bill from his wallet and laid it on the bar, relative to where he and Patrick were sitting.

Upon leaving the bar, the trio looked upon the night and observed how it had transformed the streets of Preston, Oklahoma. The luminescent street lights shone forth a colorless light onto the concrete which lay beneath it. Cars whizzed by, with their headlights creating the road that kept appearing in front of it. The sky was black, with a few white specks on the surface of the darkness. The moon shone forth towards the Earth to let Brent, Patrick, and Remi can see a few figures in the darkness.

Turning towards Brent and Patrick, Remi asked them, "Hey, you two have a ride home?"

"Not really, no," Brent replied, his eyes still trying to adjust to the darkness. Eventually they did; he then finished his statement, "I figured Henry and I would catch a cab to take us home."

"Well, there's no need for that. Here, I'll take you both home; see it as a 'Thank You' of sorts." Neither Brent nor Patrick knew what he meant by that, but they agreed to let Remi drive them back to Brent's mansion. Plus, while he did get a beer, Remi never actually drank anything at the bar. So, they figured he could play designated driver for the night. They all walked around the corner of the street in which the bar lay on and saw the parking lot; the streetlights helped illuminate the cars. As Remi was leading the two to his car, a police car whizzed past them; the red and blue lights blinded the group as they cut through the darkness like a knife through warm butter.

Reaching Remi's car, Brent looked upon the car. It looked to be a 2007 Chevrolet Aveo Sedan; Brent has some car knowledge, seeing as he was friends with Ken for quite some time. Remi dug out his keys from one of his pockets and unlocked the car. "Shotgun!" Brent yelled, as he began to enter the passenger seat. Patrick grumbled to himself, as he opened the door to the seat behind Brent. Remi, of course, got into the driver's seat, seeing as it was his car and he did offer to drive the two home. Remi put the key into the keyhole and put the car into ignition. He backed up and drove out of the parking lot, leaving only skid marks behind as he sped off into the street.

"OK, so where am I taking you two?" Remi asked, as he approached an immediate stoplight. He looked to his right to see Brent and he then looked over his shoulder to see Patrick.

Brent answered for both himself and Patrick, "Actually, Henry is staying with me for a while."

"So, you two are, like, roommates?" Remi said, constantly shifting his eyes from the two men and the stoplight.

"Uh…yeah," Patrick said, keeping up a good illusion, "You could say that."

"Here, I'll direct you to our place, Remi," Brent said, as he pointed to the stoplight in which Remi was not paying attention to at that current moment. Remi saw the loud green color emit from the stoplight, and he then proceeded to put his foot on the accelerator. "Turn left up here," Brent said, helping direct Remi to the mansion.

This went on for a good 20 minutes or so, Brent directing Remi. Patrick sat in the back seat and looked out of the window and studied the shadowed figures that sped past. When Patrick was in the back of the limo he didn't look outside of the window, because he was too intoxicated from the music. Truth of the matter is that Patrick hasn't been in a car for the past three years, the last time (before the limo) being when his older brother was in town; they met up and went out to dinner, then Matt, Patrick's brother, brought him back to his hotel and allowed him to stay the night with him, just so he could get back on his feet. Matt also left him with some money to help pay for food, and other such necessitates. The funds ran out quickly, since Patrick was never the best with handling money, but it was a nice little trip to paradise for him.

Sitting in the back seat of Remi's car, and staring out the window, Patrick spaced out and started to feel a little drowsy. He yawned, which brought him back into consciousness. In his half-awake state, Patrick realized that the car made a sharp right turn, in which Patrick followed the momentum of the car's turning, and then came to an eventual stop. Patrick looked through the seats which lie in front of him and saw a gate blocking the car's path. He then heard Remi's car door window roll down and a new voice could be heard.

"Hello. What business do you have here, sir?" asked the man to Remi.

"I'm here to drop of a friend; his name is David Webb," Remi replied. Brent winced at the sound of this, for what if the worker (who Brent recognized by his voice was Mr. Rose) told Remi that David was now Brent.

"David Webb? What the hell are you smoking'?" said Mr. Rose. He sounded like he had a cold, or he was just coming off one, as his voice was a little nasally. Makes sense, seeing as how cold it can get in that booth. After deeply inhaling, he continued with what he was saying, "I ain't ever heard of anyone by that-" he was cut off by Brent.

"Don't worry, Mr. Rose, he's with me." Brent leaned over his seat and was almost atop of Remi's lap; Brent's seatbelt kept him from going any more forward towards the booth in which Mr. Rose sat, and where Mr. Nash was earlier on in the day.

"Oh, hello sir! Sorry about that; it's my job, you know? I'll buzz you right in!" With a touch of a button, the gate unlocked and opened. Remi rolled up his window and proceeded to enter the estate, albeit very cautiously.

"What did he mean," Remi began. Brent's heart stopped, because he hadn't thought up a good lie to give Remi about Mr. Rose not knowing his old name, which Remi thought was his real name. Brent braced for impact as Remi finished his sentence, "when he said, 'sir'?" A wave of relief rushed over Brent; Patrick, however, was paying no mind to the two's conversation, for he drifted off once more.

Brent replied to Remi's answer by saying, "You'll see." Remi, not totally sure what Brent meant by that, became a bit more attentive of his surroundings.

In due time, Remi's car rounded the cul-da-sac in front of Brent's mansion. Remi's jaw dropped and almost touched the floor of his car. "You, David, you...?" Remi said, confused, as he looked upon the mansion, or at least what he could see of the mansion in the darkness. After longing at it for a few moments, his fixation now became Brent, as he studied him and imagined him being the man who owned the ginormous mansion.

Brent decided to answer Remi's question before he could even ask it, "Yup. This is my home. And yes; I'm rich." Brent smirked at this, for he loved stroking his own ego. Not in an arrogant way, mind you, but more in a sarcastic/joking way.

"....Holy crap," Remi said, still not comprehending the idea that Brent was rich, "Dude, why didn't you tell me you were loaded!"

"Well, I like to be modest about it."

Remi paused for a few seconds, still trying to wrap his mind around this. He came up with a whimsical remark, "...Mind if I borrow a few hundred bucks, buddy ol' pal?"

Brent chuckled a bit, and looked back at Patrick, whose eyelids were starting to close. "Well, I think we best get going now, Pa-Henry here is almost asleep." Brent really hoped that Remi didn't hear that, "Pa-" part.

He didn't.

"Yeah, I guess it's about time for me to hit the hay as well." Remi yawned.

Brent unbuckled himself from the confines of the car seat and spun around to yell at Patrick,

"Ohmygodthemillisonfirehurrywehavetogonow!" Patrick awoke to this immediately said, "Huh? What? Where?" Brent and Remi both laughed, and Patrick just unbuckled himself, opened the car door and tumbled out of the car and onto the ground.

Brent opened his door and stepped out onto the gravel which made up the cul-de-sac. He turned around, "Hey, Remi, thanks for taking us home."

"No problem, thanks for keeping me company tonight, and for listening to my band!" Brent turned away from Remi and was about to close the car door, but then he heard a, "Wait, hang on," release from Remi's mouth. Brent made a 180 and faced Remi again. Remi then said, "Be sure to call me sometime, OK? I want to hang out with you guys some more, and not just because you're rich!"

"Uh-huh. I'll get back to you on that, but I'm sure we'll meet up again, Remi." Remi nodded, and Brent then turned around once more and closed the car door, being very gentle with it. He didn't want to break it and pay for it, not like it would have been an issue for Brent or anything. Brent and Patrick backed up from the vicinity from the car, and Remi took off back through the area in which he drove through a little while earlier. After seeing Remi off, the two spun around to face the door. Patrick yawned loudly, and Brent opened the door to the mansion. A blinding light came out from the lobby as the door opened, and Brent and Patrick walked inside of the huge room, with Brent closing the door behind them as they walked through the entryway.

As the two men entered the lobby, Brent and Patrick both looked around the room for different reasons. Patrick, because he just wanted to see what the inside of a mansion looked like. Brent, because he was lost in a state of confusion, for his staff didn't seem to be present now. Both noticed that the lights were left on, as if someone was expecting them to return. No one was located inside the mansion, however, so someone must have done this action much earlier.

"Hey," Patrick said to Brent; Patrick still sounded drowsy, "Where is everyone? I thought you said you had people that worked for you."

Brent, finally realizing why no one was here, answered Patrick's question, "Well, everyone who works here has a shift from 6AM-6PM. I say everyone, but Ms. Fisher gets an exception, because she still goes to college. So, she has the hours of either 6AM-12PM, or 1PM-6PM. It all just depends on what's going on with her schedule that day. Digression aside, it's obviously later than 6PM, so everyone has gone home. It's just me, you, and the mansion now." Brent looked down at the floor, and noticed it wasn't as shiny as it had been this morning; it was still shiny but not as slippery. "Here," Brent said as he started to put his foot on the shiny, tiled floor, "I'll take you to a guest bedroom to sleep, for I see that you're falling asleep as I talk to you now." Patrick's head was starting to lower; Brent snapped his fingers and Patrick awoke. Brent led Patrick through the lobby to the stairs.

Patrick seemed to have a hard time climbing the set of stairs, Brent assumed it was because of his tiredness. While making his trek up the carpeted ledges, Patrick blurted out, "Hey, what did you say this, 'Ms. Fisher's', identity was, again?"

Brent reached the top of the flight of stairs, and turned around to see that Patrick was only halfway up them. Brent grunted and stopped to wait up for Patrick. He answered his question, "Her name is Hannah Fisher." He said this with some agitation in his voice.

"And you said you liked her, didn't you?" Patrick said back. He was almost to the top of the stairs; it looked as if it took almost all his energy to do this.

"What-no! I never said that!"

"Uh-huh, sure. You might not have said it, but everyone and their grandmother knows that you like her."

Brent looked away and looked at the chandelier that was hung above the lobby. It was surrounded with a cloak of glass, and it looked to be very expensive. Then again, Brent did live in a mansion. After studying the chandelier for a little while, Brent cocked his head back at Patrick's position. He noticed that Patrick was only a step or two from the top, so Brent backed up a few paces to allow Patrick the grant of entry for the top half of the mansion. Patrick reached the top, and instead of trying to catch his breath, he looked at Brent and said to him, "You never answered my question about Hannah."

"Yeah, I did, I said that I never said I liked her," Brent answered. Patrick stared at Brent. "OK, so maybe I do. A little. Listen, I don't want to talk about this now. How about I just escort you to your room?"

Patrick nodded, and Brent led Patrick to his room. The room he led him to was the room located directly to the right of Brent's room. Brent reached up above the door to the frame and pulled out a key from up top. He lowered his arm and inserted the key into the keyhole, did a little jig with his wrist, and the door opened.

Brent flicked the light switch, and the room was illuminated. The room in question looked just about the same as Brent's, with a few differences, such as a few personal items weren't lying about. Nonetheless, the room was a direct translation of Brent's.

"Well, here you are, sir," Brent said, as Patrick walked into the room.

"Wow," Patrick twirled around the room as he spoke, "This room is kick-ass!" He stopped spinning around the room and faced Brent; he walked up to him and said, "Thanks again for letting me stay with you."

"No problem, you're welcome to stay as long as you need to get you back on your feet." Brent stepped out of the room and left Patrick to himself, leaving him with Brent's words of, "Well, I'll leave you be. Good night."

"Good night," Patrick yelled back, as Brent shut the door. Brent turned to his left and reached his room, which was already unlocked. He entered his room and turned on the lights. He shut the door behind him and immediately started to undress. He pulled out the contents in his pockets and laid them all on the nightstand next to the bed, not bothering to organize them. He then took of his suit, articles of clothing at a time, and threw them into the hamper in his closet. Brent turned around to obtain his pajamas from a nearby dresser, but instead he was stopped by what was lying on his bed. It was the pair of pajamas that he wore this morning, folded on top of his bed. He found it odd, since he's never seen any clothes folded on his bed before; they've always just been put away. Brent approached the clothes and ran his hand over them. They felt clean; washed. He felt his hand stop at a certain point; like something was wrapped in the clothes. To his surprise, he found a note underneath the shirt and above the pants. In very neat and pretty handwriting it read, "Thanks for earlier". Brent's mind started to think, but then stopped; he was way too tired to figure out who wrote this. He slipped the clothes on, climbed into the bed, and unraveled the already, "made" sheets, putting himself underneath the covers. Brent almost immediately fell asleep, forgetting everything that happened to him today, from meeting Patrick to finding out about the lobotomy. He drifted off to sleep quickly, but his mind was still restless, and his dreams were not very calming, either.

Chapter 13

-Long Forgotten Sons; Rise Against-

       The ground felt wet and sticky as the shadowed man awoke. He opened his eyes to find that he was blinded by a darkness that surrounded him. He could see nothing at all, not even his own hands which he held right in front of his face. The man began to lift himself from the moist floor; he then felt a sudden sharp pain coming from his right leg. He found that the pain was coming from his kneecap. The man felt as if he was bleeding from the area in which pain emanated from. He ran his fingers over the wounded area, and then brought the fingers to his mouth, to see if he tasted blood. The sample tasted like dirt; no blood.

       The man took a cautious step forward, left foot first; he limped, due to the pain in his right knee. After a few slow, more careful steps, the man collided with something hard; a wall, or so it seemed to be. He ran his hands across the impasse; he felt a wet and sticky surface, much like the floor in which he laid on not but a few moments ago. The wall seemed to also have a rough and bumpy feel to it. The man came to the assumption that he might be inside a cave of some sort, seeing as it was so dark and the walls and floor feeling the way that they do. He put one hand against the wall as he looked around, that way his sense of direction (for lack there was) wouldn't be lost. Looking around in the darkness, the man saw in the distance, in one undistinguishable direction, a small light. It was a white light, and it didn't illuminate anything within the cave; it just looked to be there, taunting the man. He decided upon moving towards the white light, for what else did he have to do in this cave, which he wasn't even sure if it was a cave? He let go of the wall and took a step forward, towards the light. The sound of the footstep echoed off the walls of the cave and multiplied the sound to every ear-piercing extent. The exaggerated echo hurt the man's ears, but he eventually got used to it as he took more limped footsteps toward the white light.

He limped towards the light for what seemed like forever, with the entryway getting larger the closer he got. Eventually, though, the sound of his footsteps grew louder and more sporadic, as if there were other people in this cave as well. The man called out to see if anyone would reply, but the only reply he got was the excessive sounds of footsteps. With this, the man pressed on with his trek towards the light. After walking forward for a while longer, the man became infatuated with the thought of reaching the light at the end of the cave; it gave him something to strive for. Some part of him even hoped that if there were other people in the cave with him that they wouldn't get to the light before he did. He wanted to have the light rain over him first; a mental achievement is all that is was at this point. Getting to the light first wouldn't prove anything to anyone, or anything, but only to himself. It was almost as if greed was enveloping his thoughts, or maybe the sound of the footsteps was starting to get to him.

After a few more moments, the man was within 50 meters of the light. With excitement and adrenaline coursing through his veins, the man decided to swallow the pain of his right leg and hurry on towards the light. The belligerent sound of the footsteps became so deafening that the man's thoughts were completely enveloped by the sound of the footsteps; the only thing he knew and could think about now was the sound of other's determination to get what the man desired to have. He tried to shake the thought of failure, for he had come so far not to fail. He had tried too hard and been carrying along all this dead weight for what, nothing? The man tried not to fathom that thought.

He could feel the warmth of the light, for he was so close to it. The blistering sound of the footsteps now made the man lose his concentration and, in turn, he tripped on his crippled leg and collided onto the floor, taking a mouthful of the dirt and dust on the ground. The impact shot pain through the man's body, but his mind was too preoccupied with these footsteps that wouldn't stop growing louder, and closer, as well as the light which the man was so close to. His sight and thoughts began to dim, as he was on the verge of blacking out. With the last of his strength, and through excruciating pain, the man extended his right arm as far as it would stretch, in hopes of it reaching the light. At the extent of his reach, his entire hand was enveloped by the light of the outside. He raised his head to see what his hand looked like; he had been longing for the light and now that he has it he is going to look upon what gifts it brings him, even if it be small. He saw the back of his hand, which looked boney and the knuckles bulging. Tendons and bones moved as the man controlled the motions of his hand; moving each individual finger, making a fist, unclenching the fist. Little hairs could be seen on the back of his hand, which were bent by the cool breeze that lay just outside of the cave. The feeling of the refreshing breeze that hit his hand was enough to let the man die right then and there with no regrets. His arm fell limp, as the sound of the footsteps eventually claimed his thoughts once more. The man's eyes closed, with his last sight before his departure being his uncurled and limp hand in the light; a sign of freedom for him, a sign of accomplishment. A sign of hope. The footsteps then grew to their loudest yet, and the man shut down.

Chapter 14

-Closer to The Edge; 30 Seconds to Mars-

Brent awoke from his slumber to be greeted with the warming sunlight that the morning delivered through the windows in his bedroom. He blinked his eyes a few times, and rubbed the areas around his eyelids before getting up and out of bed. Brent got up and stretched his arms out. He stood next to his bed for a little while, doing a little thinking. He began to think and wonder if the events that transpired yesterday were a figment of his imagination…or were they? He always imagined scenarios in his life if he made different decisions, like if he were to cross the crosswalk at the wrong time, or something like that. His thoughts went demonic sometimes. Anyways, Brent always thought that if something traumatizing happened to him, that he would wake up a new way; scared and helpless. He always thought that if something like the morbid things he thought up were to happen to him, that it would change every aspect in his life, yet here he was, doing the same thing he's been doing for years now; still following the same routine. Brent, not wanting to think about the subject anymore, began to take off his clothes, and replaced them with jogging clothes, which he put on out of pure habit. Brent grabbed his phone and headphones from his nightstand, and looked at the picture of his family, much as he had the day before. After his longing at the picture, he then turned around, left his bedroom, and entered the hallway.

In the hallway, lights beat down on Brent. An aroma hit his senses like a freight train, and he was instantly entranced. Food sounded so good to him, and his stomach growled at him. Brent then turned and began to walk down the steps to his right. As Brent took a few steps down, he heard a closing door; the sound seemed to be emanating from behind him. Brent turned around to see what the commotion was. What he saw standing in front of the door was Patrick; he was clean shaven, no beard or mustache to speak of. He was wearing a white t-shirt, and his torn jeans that he wore yesterday. He had no beanie upon his head, which allowed for his long blonde hair to swing freely. He overall looked clean; Brent assumed that Patrick had just taken a shower. All this said, Patrick still wore his dirty shoes, though they looked as they had been washed, or at the least some water was poured over them. The mud and dirt was no longer on them. Brent stood on the stairs and waited for Patrick to catch up with him; he didn't question where Patrick got a utensil in which to shave, let alone how he did it.

"Morning, Patrick," Brent said to him, as Patrick approached.

"Morning, Brent," Patrick replied. He sniffed the air. "What is that I smell…?" Patrick thought aloud.

"Breakfast," Brent replied, smug.

The two then walked down the stairs and into the dining hall, which was connected to the kitchen. The scent of food was now at its strongest point, as Brent and Patrick approached the long table. Brent saw sitting around the table, Mrs. Green, Mrs. Bayer, and S. Mrs. Green and Mrs. Bayer were talking about something, but neither Brent nor Patrick could tell what they were talking about, though Patrick was still trying to figure out who these new people were. Mrs. Green looked at Brent and Patrick, "Oh, hello, Mr. McIlrath, joining us for breakfast today, are you?"

Brent chuckled at this. "Yeah, I'm not missing out on breakfast today. What are we having?"

"French Toast." Mrs. Green stood up from her seat. "I think I'll go ahead and distribute the food to everyone." She looked at Patrick, with confusion written all over her face. "Will…he be joining us, too?" She looked at Brent for an answer.

"Yes, he will," Brent said back. He turned towards Patrick, whom was on his right. "I forgot to introduce him. This is-" he was cut off.

"Patrick Armstrong, nice to meet you." Patrick held out his hand, to politely shake hands with Mrs. Green.

She just said back, real awkwardly, "Shaniqua Green. I would shake your hand, but I don't want to have to wash up again."

Patrick took his hand back. "Ah, OK. Well, nice to meet you, Shaniqua."

"Just call me Mrs. Green, Mr. Armstrong." With that, Mrs. Green walked into the kitchen to get the food. Brent and Patrick advanced towards the dining room table. They sat down in two seats that were adjacent to one another.

Patrick looked around the table, at Mrs. Bayer and S, who sat on opposite to Brent and Patrick. He gave a nervous smile to both and looked upon Mrs. Bayer and said, "Hi."

"Hello," she replied, shyly. "Oh, where are my manners?" she continued, "My name is McKayla Bayer, but you can just call me Mrs. Bayer."

"Name's Patrick Armstrong, glad to meet your acquaintance." Patrick didn't try and shake hands with Mrs. Bayer; he didn't want to feel like an idiot again.

About this time, Mrs. Green walked back into the dining room, with five plates in one hand, and a little larger plate in the other hand. The larger of the plates had pieces of French Toast on it. She laid the larger plate down on the table, and passed the smaller plates around so that everyone had a plate sitting in front of them. Mrs. Green then walked around to everyone and dropped off two pieces of toast on everyone's plate. "Thank you," said each of the people who sat at the table when Mrs. Green gave them their food. When Mrs. Green finished distributing breakfast, she, too, sat down and put two pieces of toast on her own plate. As she finished putting the food on her own plate, she dug into the toast, and soon everyone else followed into theirs.

Patrick, naturally, was the first to finish his meal. He wasn't completely full, but he'd lived being not completely full for years now; he was used to the feeling. The taste of the food he was eating, though, was much better than much of the food he had been living off. It was syrupy-tasting to him, which he didn't really mind. Patrick was never too keen on syrup, but he didn't really care at this moment. It was better than starving, he thought. He ended up sitting there for a little while, not too long, as he waited for everyone else to finish.

Promptly, the other people sitting around the table finished their breakfast, and Mrs. Green walked around and picked up the plates, all with remnants of food on them. While Mrs. Green walked into the kitchen, and began to wash the plates, Brent asked both S and Mrs. Bayer, "Hey, where's Ms. Fisher at this morning?"

S shook his head and shrugged. Mrs. Bayer responded, "She's working the late shift today, sir."

"Yeah, I guess that makes sense. Should have thought of that," Brent replied.

Patrick looked upon S and Mrs. Bayer while Brent talked with them. They were consistently shifting their eyes towards him, to get a good look of him; they tried to not make it too obvious, but they failed. Patrick didn't bring attention to this, but he did think it was rather suspicious how often they glanced at him.

After a few moments of silence, Brent broke it by saying, "Well, I should probably start getting ready…Patrick, come with me, please." Brent and Patrick then both stood up and walked out of the dining room and into the kitchen. Brent yelled, "Thank you for the toast, Mrs. Green; it was very good!" to Mrs. Green as they passed her; she was still washing the plates, though it looked as if she was almost done.

"Yes, thank you," Patrick said as he, too, walked past Mrs. Green.

"My pleasure, Mr. McIlrath and Mr. Armstrong!" she replied, over the sound of rushing water.

Walking into the main lobby, Brent turned to Patrick and said, "So, hey," Patrick's attention was taking by Brent. He continued, "As I said yesterday, I jog every morning, so I wanted to ask you if you wanted to join me?"

"Yeah, sure. It probably wouldn't hurt to run today, either," Patrick replied.

"OK, cool." Brent looked at Patrick's current clothing. "You, uh, sure you want to run in that?"

"Trust me," Patrick reassured Brent, "I'm used to running in worse conditions. I'm pretty sure a white t-shirt and jeans won't be the end of me."

"Well, if you're sure..." Brent said, not totally liking the idea. From that, Brent turned and led Patrick out the front doors. The door opened much easier than it had the previous day, for the wind had died down. The outside air, while stagnate, was still a bit frigid.

The cul-de-sac looked just about the same as it had the day before; the American flag was still flying high in the air, the trees dances in time with the wind. Patrick thought this was a beautiful sight, and Brent could tell. "Wait until we get to running, then you'll see some sights," Brent told him, and Brent began to jog. Patrick's mind didn't register Brent running ahead for a few seconds, and then when he finally did notice, he bolted after him.

While on their run, Patrick's senses took in everything about the path; from the lush forest setting to the open-lake area. Patrick was always the kind of person who if he went on a nature walk, he would absorb, dissect, and appreciate every tiny detail. He was always amazed by what nature provided us with, and now was no exception. Patrick also loved to run because of the sheer fact that it gave him a chance to clear his mind, and do some thinking. He often lost himself in thought and bewilderment while running with Brent, only to be alerted back to his senses when he found himself almost colliding with a tree. He then got himself back on the path and continued to run in a straight line, until his thoughts enveloped his conscience, that is.

Upon approaching the end of the path, Brent sped up, leaving Patrick in the dust. Brent ran up towards the gate and touched it with his palm, and then turned around and waited for Patrick to catch up.

"Dick," Patrick said towards Brent when he was within earshot. Brent just shrugged his shoulders and chuckled.

"Ey, who's there?" asked a familiar voice, or at least to Brent it was. The voice emerged itself out of the "tollbooth". It was Mr. Nash. "Ah, 'ello, Mr. McIlrath! Who's dis fella, 'ere?"

"Oh, why," Brent turned from Mr. Nash to Patrick, "this is my friend Patrick Armstrong."

"Hi," Patrick said as he outstretched an open hand towards Mr. Nash. Patrick was breathing heavily, along with Brent, from their run.

"Mr. Nash took Patrick's hand. "Ello der, lad! My name's Jon Nash, but you can just call me Mr. Nash; just don't call me Willy," Mr. Nash gave a long stare at Brent. Brent burst out into laughter, while Patrick just stood there confused. He never found out what that was about. Mr. Nash then continued, "You know, I don't think I've seen you around 'ere before."

"That's because you haven't. I-uh," Brent started to say, but then tripped over his own words. He looked at Patrick who just gave him an unsure look at what to say, "I ran into him yesterday, and we haven't seen each other in so long that I invited him to the mansion for the night."

"Ah, OK then!" exclaimed Mr. Nash, "I believe ya."

"Well we best be headed back to the mansion now," Brent said, "See you again, Mr. Nash!"

"It was nice meeting you, er, Mr. Nash," Patrick added.

"The pleasure was all mine, Mr. Armstrong. See ya!" yelled Mr. Nash. Brent and Patrick then disappeared into the path again and they finished their run.

Upon returning to the mansion, Brent and Patrick both resided to their rooms and decided to take showers. They were both kind of sweaty, and they were planning on seeing Kevin at 3:00PM anyway. Brent, once he finished his shower, dried himself off and put on an elegant-looking blue colored suit. Patrick ended up wearing an orange colored t-shirt (one that Brent let him borrow) underneath his slightly-less cleaned, albeit still dirty-green jacket that he wore the day prior. He wasn't wearing his green beanie, for he wanted to let his hair dry. Plus, he cleaned his beanie earlier that morning, so he also wanted that to dry as well.

Once both were done taking their showers and getting dressed, the two met outside in the hallway, just outside of their rooms. Brent looked upon Patrick's clothing, as he did the same with Brent. Brent then asked, "Is this the second shower you took today?"

"Dude, I haven't had an actual shower in God knows when…if I had an excuse, I'd take a third shower!" Patrick chuckled a little as he replied.

Brent let out a little laugh in return, and then said, "Hey, we have some time; let me show you around the mansion a bit."

"Sure!" Patrick sounded as giddy as an eight-year old at an amusement park.

Brent then showed Patrick all around the mansion. He showed him the bedrooms, including his own room, and Brent also could see Patrick's room. It looked vacant, apart from the drying articles of clothing strung all around. After the bedrooms, Brent led Patrick downstairs and gave him a redefined look at the kitchen and dining rooms; Mrs. Green wasn't in either of these rooms, though. Brent then led Patrick through the lobby, the recreational room (or living room as Brent likes to refer to it as), and the trophy room. Brent didn't show Patrick the "behind-the-scenes" rooms, only the highlights. Oddly, though, Brent didn't see any of his workers when he was showing Patrick around the house. He paid no mind to it, however.

Patrick, during all of this, was just amazed and astonished by what he was seeing. He felt as if he was touring a museum. Patrick did notice, however, there was a copious number of pictures of Brent and Brent's parents along the walls of the mansion. This caused a chain-reaction of memories to start flooding into Patrick's mind; some of them he wished he hadn't remembered.

Brent's tour around the mansion ended with a door that seemed to be hidden in the lobby. Brent put his hand on the doorknob, and Patrick asked, "So where does this door lead us to?"

"For right now," Brent said back, "nowhere important," and Brent turned the handle. A light shone in on the lobby, as Patrick's and Brent's eyes dilated. What Patrick saw outside looked to be a mixed setting; directly in front of him was a dirt-covered wasteland, but further out was a beautiful green backyard-area.

"Yeah," Brent burst out, as he and Patrick stepped out form the doorframe and onto a small patch of concrete that lay before the dirt began to cover the earth. Brent shut the door behind them, and continued his statement, "This is where I plan on putting that bowling alley; the one I was talking to Jaime about yesterday, remember?"

"Yeah, I remember..." Patrick said, but his mind wasn't thinking about that now. He finally couldn't keep his thoughts to himself anymore, and blurted out, "Hey Brent," Brent turned to face Patrick, while he continued, "When we were walking through the mansion, I noticed you had a lot of pictures of you, as well as your parents..." Brent's mood dropped as Patrick went on, "And from that, some memories came rushing back to me...one of them was the death of your parents."

Brent looked hurt and scarred by that comment, and just broke eye contact with Patrick and looked at the ground. Patrick began to wonder if he should have even brought that topic up, but it was already too late to turn back. "Hey, listen," Patrick started, sounding very sympathetic, "I'm sorry about bringing it up; I should have just kept that to myself."

"No, it's fine," Brent whimpered, starting to regain his posture once more, "In a way, I'm glad you brought it up. It proves to me that maybe my recollection of that event isn't augmented. If that's the case..." Brent broke off and inhaled the clean air of the outside. He seemed to be lost in thought, and Patrick had no intention of pressing him any further than he already has. After some time, Brent looked back up at Patrick and said, "Never mind. I'd rather not talk about this subject for the moment, if that's OK."

"Fine by me," Patrick said back with a little whimsy, hoping to lift the mood a little bit. He didn't.

Brent then continued, "We need to focus on what to do next right now, opposed to my past."

Patrick nodded, and the two stood in silence for a few moments. You could almost feel the tension that lingered in the air.

"Well I guess that's the end of here, then," Brent said, breaking the ice. He then turned around and opened the door that led back to the lobby. Brent walked through the door, with Patrick following closely behind; Patrick shut the door behind the two of them.

The rest of the day came sluggishly, for 2:30PM seemed like such a long time away. Brent and Patrick spent the rest of the day just listening to music that the two gushed over, watching TV, and just talking about random things. At lunch, Brent's staff peer-pressured Brent and Patrick into telling them how they met up yesterday. They skipped the details about them finding out they were lobotomized; *"No need to drag them into this,"* Brent thought.

After lunch was a lot of nothing, basically consisting of what Brent and Patrick were doing before lunch. At around 1PM, or so, Ms. Fisher walked into the mansion to report for duty. Brent got up from the couch he was glued to so he could greet her. Patrick also joined along, since he hasn't really seen this famous, "Hannah Fisher" yet.

Ms. Fisher looked rather laid back, which was fitting seeing as she just came from college. Her brown hair was down, and not pinned up like it usually was when she was working. She had on a black long-sleeved shirt, and jeans, and she also bore a pink bag (that was more like a satchel) which was draped across her chest. Brent thought the bag made her look more dignified, in a way.

"Good afternoon, Ms. Fisher!" said Brent, seeming overly happy about it.

"Oh, hello Mr. McIlrath!" Ms. Fisher brushed hair out of her face, and fixed her glasses. "Um...and who might you be, if you don't mind me asking?" Ms. Fisher asked, whilst sporting a confused look on her face as Patrick entered the scene.

"Oh yes: Ms. Fisher, this is my friend, Patrick Armstrong. Patrick, this is Ms. Fisher," Brent explained, though he kept a close watch on Patrick; he was ready to pounce on him if he decided to say something ignorant.

"Pleasure to meet your acquaintance, Mr. Armstrong," Ms. Fisher said, extending out her hand.

Patrick met her hand, and said, "The pleasure is all mine. And please, call me Patrick."

"Will do! And you may call me Hannah if you'd like, Patrick," she turned to Brent, "That goes for you too."

"Sure thing, Hannah," Brent and Patrick said, almost in unison. Hannah laughed a little bit, and then said, "Well I should probably go and get ready. Where should I report to, Mr. McIlrath?"

"Just go get dressed up and find Mrs. Bayer; she'll tell you what you should do today."

"OK, thank you Mr. McIlrath! Nice to meet you, Patrick!" Hannah then walked past the two and out of the lobby. Patrick then looked to Brent, with a giddy look on his face, and a smile ten miles wide.

"What?" asked Brent; he couldn't get over Patrick's face.

"Nothing. She's cute," Patrick said back. He was grinning as if he still had more he wanted to say.

"Thanks, I guess," Brent responded.

"I just didn't know you were into shorter women, though, Brent,"

"*There it is...*" Brent thought to himself. "Oh, shut up," he retorted.

"She's nice and all, don't get me wrong, but she's tiny!"

"Shut up." Brent turned around and started walking away, towards the direction Hannah went.

"You two make a cute couple!" Patrick yelled at him.

Brent, whilst walking away, held up his middle finger, but not so much in a hateful way; more of in a comedic way. Patrick laughed, and then walked back into the living room; Hannah soon emerged from the room she was in (faculty room). She just looked at Brent and laughed a bit, for she heard a little of what the two were bickering about. Brent just blushed and accompanied Hannah in her grand search for Mrs. Bayer.

Eventually, 2:30PM rolled around. Brent and Patrick went into their rooms and tidied themselves up a bit: Brent just combed his hair and covered up any facial blemishes; Patrick combed his hair also, but he put his green beanie over top of it, so that rendered his efforts basically pointless. Brent, after the two were ready to leave, led Patrick out of the parking garage. Brent then grabbed his keys for his car, and led Patrick to the car.

"This is a pretty sweet ride you got here," Patrick told him after the two were comfortable inside of the automobile.

"Thanks," is all Brent said back. He then started the car and proceeded to drive on towards Preston High School. The two never spoke a word in the car ride there; they were too caught up in the questions they wanted answered and what they are going to talk with Kevin about.

Chapter 15

-Everlong; Foo Fighters-

After a short, but silent, car ride, Brent and Patrick arrived at Preston High School. Brent started to pull into the parking lot, which had a few cars strewn around it, and eventually came to a stop. Before getting out of the car, Brent and Patrick looked towards the school; the outside was made of red brick, which Patrick, being the more artistic of the duo, found to add to the nostalgia of the place. The words, "PRESTON HIGH SCHOOL" were written in huge white-bolded letters, and hung above the doors of the school.

As soon as Brent and Patrick's feet touched the pavement of the parking lot, memories started rushing back to them. They weren't anything of major importance: Brent recalled eating lunch with all his friends at the lunch tables, and how they always messed with one another during that time. He recalled one time where he and his friends peer-pressured one of his friends, Evan, into eating a package of wasabi. Brent smiled upon that recollection.

Patrick remembered how, during the times in which the school's play was relevant, he, Brent, and a couple of their friends would skip a few of their classes every day to help paint the play's set. They all, while paying attention to what they were doing, would talk about their days so far, complain about how much homework a teacher is giving them, exchange gossip they've heard, etc. Patrick also smiled a little at this recollection.

As the two continued to walk into the school, their memories kept coming back to them; none of them pertinent to their lobotomies or what the two really wanted to know, but it was nice to be remembering some happy memories for once, the two later concluded. It was a nice little break from the craziness that life's thrown at them for the past two days.

They walked into their old High School like they were top of the walk; their heads held high, and their spirits to match. There was something about going back to a place you are so familiar with when you're older, they thought. The two found themselves in the cafeteria as soon as they entered the building. They made a sharp left, and then another, and were now in the main office. There was a secretary working diligently, typing who-knows-what into the computer she sat behind. Brent approached her; the secretary glanced over and saw him. She turned from her work to meet Brent and said, "Good afternoon! How may I help, sir?"

"Hi, yes," Brent said, sounding a little more assertive than usual, "We would like to see Mr. Long, please."

"Mr. Long is in room 216. I'm sure he's free right now, so you can probably go meet with him now if you'd like," the secretary replied.

"OK, thank you," Brent said happily, and then he and Patrick walked out of the office and headed towards room 216. They knew exactly where it was; it was their old chemistry classroom.

Walking through the halls was almost like a trip down memory Long for the two. They saw the locker the two shared all throughout High School: Locker #545. For shits and giggles, Patrick tried to open the locker; he suddenly remembered the combination for no real reason. He tried the code. Nothing.

"They must have changed the code since we were here last," Patrick finally concluded.

"Yeah, no shit. I told you that! If they didn't, people like us could come through and pilfer a kid's stuff," Brent added. Patrick shrugged in agreement. The duo then just decided to just stop dicking around and go see Kevin now.

The school was still the same as it was when Brent and Patrick went to school there. The walls were still sour-cream white, the floors stripped with white and green. It wasn't as unpleasant as Brent and Patrick remembered it being. Perhaps that's because they haven't seen it in so long; maybe the fact of seeing these colors again relaxed the two, in a sense. Either way, it made making their way to Kevin, while it really didn't take that long, feel like forever. Memories kept flooding back to them, some just pieces of moments.

One second Brent could remember him and one of his old girlfriends walking together down the hall, while in an instant that could lead to Brent walking through the school's library searching for a book. Patrick's mental state was just the same: One moment he remembers conversations he had with friends in his English class, then the next he's recalling a fight he got in during his Freshman year.

Soon, Brent and Patrick reached the science hallway. It was more a science wing, because it branched out from the business hallway. Kevin's room, if their memory served them right, was the last door on the left. They were correct about that.

Walking through the science hallway, Patrick saw some posters drawn by kids; the posters were hanging from the walls. They were all science fiction stories: The Amory Wars, House of Gold and Bones, Kilroy Was Here, The Wall, and a few others were visible as well. Patrick saw them and smiled; it brought him a little joy to know that he knew of these stories that High School students were reading, and learning about. Although, Patrick wasn't too familiar with House of Gold and Bones; that one was new.

After admiring the surprisingly beautifully-drawn posters on the wall, Patrick broke out of his spell and remembered the real mission ahead. Brent then looked to his left and saw a glass casing next to the room before Kevin's. In it were two student-made rollercoasters; one had a zoo theme, while the other focused more around bowling, or so it looked to be. Brent then recalled when he was in his Physics class when he and three other people had to make a rollercoaster. For some reason, he recalled all three of their names: Brandon Stringer, Ben Huff, and Alyssa Ikkin. Brent wondered how those three were doing, as he continued to remember the assignment. It was strange to think about how all four of them went their separate ways; in high school, all information was condensed. Out in the real world, though, that info gets more spread out, and only a few people then know it.

Brent remembered that the rollercoaster was sports-related, and that the rollercoaster itself had two loops and a corkscrew, and then still went on. He remembered that they won 1st place up against all the other coasters; he recalled how happy they all were at the time. Brent kind of wished he could relive that feeling sometime soon. A feeling that nothing else mattered, and all his worries were gone for a few moments.

After the memories pieced themselves together, Brent and Patrick found themselves standing outside Kevin's door. "Mr. Long – 216" was written above the door. Patrick then opened the door and the two entered, both hoping they walk out of this with good intentions, as well as some leads.

Kevin's classroom looked very clean and orderly, Brent and Patrick noticed as they glanced around the room real fast. Kevin looked up from his stack of papers with a red pen in hand, and greeted the two: "By God, if it isn't David and Henry!"

"Hey, Kevin," Brent and Patrick both said in unison. They looked around for a second or two to study the room.

The contents in the classroom verified that Kevin was an astronomy teacher. Posters of the solar system and other galaxies were hung all throughout the room. Styrofoam versions of planets were strung form the ceiling and draped around portions of the room. There were tables throughout the class, all of them with four chairs; one chair for each side. Brent noticed on one of the walls was a poster that read, "All-Star Students – Perfect Scores". There was only one name on that list: Andy Madison. That name seemed familiar to him. *"Did I know a Madison when I went here?"* Brent asked himself; he then soon disregarded it and moved on.

Quickly after scanning the room, Kevin soon said, "Aw, come on! You can look around the room later. Come on, sit! Sit!" He pointed to two chairs that were around a table nearest to him. Brent and Patrick picked up the chairs and moved them to face Kevin, and placed them in front of his desk. The two then sat down.

Kevin's desk looked like a mess, which seemed odd, because Patrick recalled him always being a very organized person. Plus, the rest of the room looked to be tidy. Papers cluttered Kevin's desk, as well as a few pens and a couple pencils. A red stapler was on the corner of the desk, along with a box of paperclips and a roll of tape. A widescreen computer was located behind the stapler and other such items. A corded phone was located near the computer; the school's extension line came down from it, and into the wall. Lastly, a mug of water sat on top of a thick book, titled, *Astronomy: Teacher's Edition.*

"So how have you two been doing?" Kevin asked. He seemed giddy.

"I've been better, to be honest," Patrick replied first. He rubbed his hand over top his beanie as he said this. He was trying to be vague with his answer.

"I've been doing OK, I guess," was Brent's response. He, too, was trying to be vague. Brent then asked, "How have things been with you, Kevin?"

"I've been doing pretty well, actually!" he replied. "Yeah, I love this job; income might not be the best, but that's fine. Still single, but that's cool; I'll find someone eventually, right?" He laughed. "Overall, I'm happy where I'm at now."

"Well that's good to hear," Brent said back. There was a moment of silence, which gave Brent to kind of "size up" Kevin himself.

Kevin looked to be the same as Brent, shape-wise. He looked to be about the same weight and height, too. His eyes were green, and his face looked rather elongated; he was clean-shaven as well. His brown hair was short, and looked to be fixed, like he put gel in it. Kevin also looked rather muscular; Brent looked at Kevin's shirt, which read, "Preston Panthers: Varsity Football". Brent correlated the muscles to that. Behind Kevin, Brent noticed a black jacket hung over his chair.

After the little bit of silence, Kevin broke it by asking the two, "So, uh, do you two have a woman, or what?" Kevin leaned back in his chair, almost as if he was anticipating a long story up ahead. My, how he would get to hear some story by the end of the group's conversation...

"Um…" Brent was the first to say something. He said this almost involuntary; he was thinking about Hannah the whole time, but he didn't want to jump to any conclusions and be forced to make up stories. Would he have loved to talk to Kevin about Hannah? Hell yeah! But did he really want to? Not really, no. So instead he answered with, "Not yet, Kevin. Not yet…" Brent thought after he said this, *"Good. Vague and to the point, just what I wanted."*

Patrick's turn came, and he answered normally with, "Me neither. At least, not yet, yeah."

"Looks like we're in the same boat then, huh?" Kevin said, chuckling. Patrick smirked, and Brent just looked unaffected by it. Kevin then stopped chuckling, and started a new topic, "So I got a call from Remi this morning and he said he talked to you guys last night?"

Brent responded with, "Yes, we sure did. Still the same crazy man we know and love. He's actually the one who told us you were an astronomy teacher."

"He did, did he?" Kevin asked. Kevin looked to be a little proud that someone's gloating about him behind his back.

"So, what's it like, being an astronomy teacher?" Patrick asked Kevin, hoping to break a little tension.

"I really like it," Kevin responded, beginning his story, "I get to preach what I love, so that's a plus. Grading papers is no fun, though." Kevin broke off. He spoke quickly when he was talking about things that excited him. He took a second to kind of catch himself.

"Yeah, I can imagine," Patrick said, sounding not totally convinced; maybe it was more of him not caring. Either one.

The room feel silent once more, and Kevin looked like he was "eyeing-up" Brent and Patrick. The two felt a little uneasy about this; Kevin eventually said, "OK, the look's right on your guys' faces."

"Excuse me?" Brent questioned.

"Well," Kevin leaned back in his chair, "going back to what I said earlier, about Remi calling me and all, when I got the call from him, I kind of thought that it was strange how you two, whom I haven't heard word from in so long, would suddenly meet Remi. Now that's just coincidence, I get that, but then you two decide that you would come and see me, just because, 'Why not?'" Kevin leaned in real close. He said, almost in a whisper, "Listen, you guys are here for some alternate reason other than to just 'catch up'. So, go ahead, talk to me; I'm all ears." Kevin leaned back in his chair again. He also cleaned up some papers from his desk and created a new pile of crap off to the side of the desk.

Brent and Patrick looked at each other and exchanged looks. The two had the same idea, though. They both decided that they were going to talk with Kevin about what they found out yesterday, as well as their journey thus far. Kevin was always someone whom the two trusted, and he never leaked secrets to anyone. He was always someone who seemed to always know what to do. It was almost as if he had a plan for any given situation that could possibly surface.

So, then Brent and Patrick told Kevin all that they knew, and what all they learned within the past day.

Chapter 16

-Way Away; Yellowcard-

"Wow," is all Kevin said when Brent and Patrick told them of their story.

"Trust me, we know," said Brent. The two told him of everything; backstabbing Ken, Jaime and his acting distant, and what all else they've kind of figured out on their own.

Kevin started to scratch his head. "I'm just trying to make sense of it all..."

"It's not as easy as it may seem," Patrick said, sounding a little sarcastic.

"And this is all true...Patrick?" Kevin said, being very careful with the way he said, "Patrick".

"We think so, yes," he replied.

"Well, I'm almost thinking that maybe Jaime was right about the whole, 'Ken might be messing with you guys' thing," Kevin said back, still trying to see if there's some rhyme or reason behind all this.

"Nope," Brent replied, "You called us David and Henry when we walked in; Remi also called us by that. The only people who called us by our new names have been the two people who were, supposedly, in on what happened.

"Jaime could also be a part of this, 'prank'!" Kevin yelled, sounding sort of angry. He wasn't angry at anyone , but more at the situation, and how powerless he was.

Patrick replied to Kevin's sudden outburst: "Jaime didn't seem like he was a part of just some joke. He made it seem much more serious than that. If it is some great joke-a cruel one, mind you- then he has us fooled."

"Plus," Brent joined in, "My memories of me are encrypted with Brent McIlrath. I have no recollection of being David Webb. Walking through this High School, bits and pieces of memories came back to me, but that's it. A few other things trigger memoires of my past life, too. But it wasn't until I saw Patrick again that things I've been passing for years just started to give me memories; as if Patrick was the key to my mental lock, or something."

"Me as well," Patrick said back. He looked at Brent for a few seconds, and then looked back to Kevin. "Plus, when we were talking with Remi, he called us David and Henry as if we were those people our entire lives. You called us David and Henry too, Kevin." Kevin bit his lip to that. "In addition to," Patrick bent over and showed Kevin his scar, "Brent and I both have this scar; a lobotomy scar."

"It all just adds up," Brent finished what Patrick was saying.

Kevin just sighed heavily to this and eventually said, "I guess." He sounded almost defeated. Didn't Brent and Patrick know the feeling...

A quick burst of silence spread across the room. Kevin eventually asked the two, "You two remember Chris, right?"

"Yeah," Brent and Patrick both replied at the same time.

"OK, good." Kevin's eyes looked around his room for a few seconds, and he soon fixated them on Brent and Patrick and continued his thought: "The reason I bring him up is because I remember a while back, Chris came into my class, much like you two did, and told me some gibberish that I didn't understand. He said something about losing his memory, and if I knew anything about it. I told him, 'No', because I, obviously, didn't know anything about him losing his memory. Up until that point, he hadn't spoken three words to me since High School...Anyways, the point of this being, he told me to call him if anything came by me that had to do with memory loss, or something like that, I can't totally remember the conversation that well." Kevin ripped off a piece of paper and grabbed one of his pens that was assorted all-about his desk. He started to write something down on it. While he was doing this, he continued to say, "I didn't really pay much mind to what Chris told me at the time; I thought he was crazy, to be honest with you." Kevin then quickly finished what he was writing down and handed it to Brent. Brent looked down at the paper; it was an address and a phone number.

"An address?" Brent didn't really read what was on the paper, at first. He wanted to know what the purpose of the note was before he committed to learning it.

"Yes, it's Chris's address, as well as his phone number. Now while I'm still not totally sure what Chris's...talk...was about, I figured you can go talk to him, if you want to." Kevin leaned forward a bit.

Brent looked down at the note, and read it:

"1423 Ranch Blvd
#785-345-6257"

Patrick questioned the note a little bit. "How do you know this off the top of your head, Kevin?" he asked.

"I don't even know," Kevin said back. He started to laugh a little, "It's just one of those dumb things you remember, I guess!"

Patrick still wasn't totally convinced by this, but he bought it. He understood the feeling; some things you just remember for no real reason at all.

Kevin continued on, "Chris currently lives in Lawrence, Kansas. I know it's a while away, but a few other people live there as well, coincidentally."

"Really?" Brent pondered, "Like who?"

Kevin's eyes looked up at the ceiling as he remembered, and said off the names, "Well let's see...there's Chris, of course, Polly, Nick...I think Emily might live there, too, but I'm not totally sure on that." Kevin became silent for a little bit. "I think that's all, actually. Or, at least, the one's I've been in contact with.

Brent looked at Patrick for a moment, and Patrick just nodded his head in response. They were both thinking the same thing.

"Thank you for the address and number, Kevin!" exclaimed Brent, "We'll be sure to check it out."

"No problem!" Kevin replied with a sense of excitement. He continued, "Anything I can do to help you guys out."

"Well we appreciate it," Brent said as he and Patrick began to stand up from their chairs. They put the chairs back in their original locations; almost as if they were never moved to begin with. Brent and Patrick then went back up toward Kevin' Brent also realized he was still holding the note Kevin gave him. Brent then quickly shoved the note into his pocket.

Kevin stood up from his chair and extended his hand. "Hey, thanks for coming to see me today, and for telling me for what's been going on with you two," he said with happiness in his tone.

Brent shook his hand. "No problem."

Patrick, too, shook Kevin's hand. "Yeah, you're welcome. Thank you for listening to us; It's nice to have someone else to talk to about this, you know?"

Kevin smirked and sheepishly held back a smile. "Just know, you two, that I'm always here to help; I may not be much help, but I'm here if you need me."

"We'll be sure to get in contact with you soon and tell you info as we come across it," Brent told Kevin very quickly.

"OK. Oh, wait, hold up!" Kevin said, and then ripped off another piece of paper and wrote something down on it. He handed the note to Brent. "Here's my phone number, in case you want it."

"Yeah, sure. Thanks!" Brent took the paper, read it real fast, and stuffed it in his pocket with the previous note.

The men said their goodbyes once more, and Brent and Patrick left the classroom swiftly. They shut the door behind them and didn't look back. The two didn't really talk walking out of school for two reasons. One: they felt it a little awkward talking about the situation in an empty school with no one (seemingly) around. Two: the duo was too eager to get their adventure started; thoughts came faster to them than words did.

During the car ride, back to the mansion is the only time the two talked to each other about the matter at hand.

Brent started by saying, "So we're both in agreement that we're going to Lawrence, then?"

"Hell yeah," replied Patrick sounding excited, albeit quietly. He shifted around in his seat a little.

"You cool if we leave tomorrow morning?"

"I condone that, actually." Patrick sighed. "I just need to know the truth...even if I don't really want to know it."

Brent shook his head. The car became silent, other than the noises from outside. Brent came to a stop at a stoplight.

"You know," Patrick started to say, "I was thinking about something when we were talking with Kevin."

Brent's ears perked up.

"The people who call us David and Henry don't know what happened to us..." Brent agreed with him. Patrick then went on, "And the ones who call us Brent and Patrick do know what happened to us..." Brent, again, agreed with him. Patrick continued, "Well...that got me thinking. And, well..." Patrick grew silent. After a few seconds, he finished his thought: "All your workers, they called you Brent; never David, right?"

"Nope, not onc-" the realization hit Brent like a freight train. He never really thought about it until Patrick brought it up. He lost himself in thought on the road, and was starting to veer off it. Patrick reached over and grabbed the wheel from him, and put the car back on the road. Brent then kind of started to pay more attention to the road ahead of him, but his mind still went on thinking about what Patrick just brought up.

"*They've always called me Brent...never called me David...does that mean...?*" Brent thought to himself. He then said, aloud, "Patrick, you are a goddamned detective!"

Patrick said, very conceded, "Well, I try."

"Yeah, no," Brent thought aloud, "I never put two-and-two together before. Yeah, maybe do they know what happened to us?" Patrick shrugged. Brent then sighed and said, "Why would they never have told me anything? Why have they always kept this a secret from me?" Brent paused. "Was that maybe for the best...?" He then looked off the road for a second, and looked at Patrick. "I'm holding a meeting tonight and I'm going to address the issue. You're going to be there for morale support, OK?"

"Sure thing," Patrick agreed, "I wasn't going to miss it anyway. I want to know about this no more than you do." He paused and then added, "I need to keep you in line, anyway."

Brent laughed, and the car fell silent once more. Brent turned left and was in front of the gates that led to the mansion. Brent and Patrick spoke little until the meeting that night.

The rest of the day came along sluggishly, as the two were meeting tonight for a romantic date with Brent's staff; except it wasn't going to be very romantic...or date-worthy. Brent and Patrick just kind of hung around for the rest of the day listening to music, watching a little TV, and watching the Kansas Basketball game that was on that night. At dinner, everyone was fixed Spaghetti and Meatballs by Mrs. Green; Brent and Patrick just picked at the food. They were too nervous of what was to come that night; too eager as well.

Eventually, 7PM came. As everyone started to head towards the faculty room to gather their things, Brent stood before all them and said loudly, "Excuse me, everyone!" They all listened to him. "Hi," Brent said, nervously, "Um...before everyone leaves for the day, could I get you all to meet in the living room, please! Thank you!" From that announcement, everyone turned around and started heading to the living room. Brent let S, Mrs. Green, and Mrs. Bayer go into the living room; everyone he wanted to talk to about this. When Hannah passed by Brent, he put out his hand, wrapped it around her shoulder and held her back. He then said to her, "Op-op-op, I want you to stay behind."

"What? Why?" she sounded very disappointed by this, and a little worried. "You're not...going to talk bad about me to everyone, are you?"

"What? No, God, no!" Brent defended himself rather quickly. "I just need to talk to them about something that doesn't really concern you, is all; nothing bad about you at all, trust me!" He leaned in real close to Hannah and whispered, "You're too perfect to talk bad about!"

Hannah shied away and blushed. "You're too sweet, Mr. McIlrath..."

"Oh, please," Brent said, "Call me Brent from now on, OK, Hannah?"

"Uh, yeah, sure…Brent!" Hannah said. She laughed a little bit, and Brent laughed along with her.

"Anyways, go ahead on into the faculty room and get your stuff collected. Hang out in there until everyone else starts to come out of the meeting, OK?"

Hannah shook her head nervously and said she understood her orders. She then went into the faculty room, and Brent turned and headed to face-off with a truth that he doesn't really want told.

A loud chatter smashed into Brent as he waltzed into the living room. Everyone was sitting/standing on or around the couch, facing towards the TV. Brent positioned himself in front of the TV, with Patrick standing a few feet off to his left; morale support.

"Hello everyone," Brent started off his speech, "So I gathered everyone in here to talk about something that, quite frankly, needs to be addressed." Everyone's ears in the crowd perked up, for they were expecting to hear bad news about someone or something. Brent went on, "Now, I just want to thank all of you so much for all the work you've done for me; I know I might not say it a whole lot, but I am very appreciative of everything you do for me.

", I feel like I can trust you all with anything, and I feel like you can trust me with anything. Well, today an idea popped into my head that made me feel like that connection was corrupt. There's something that you all are hiding from me, and I know what it is; that's the whole reason I called everyone here right now."

All the staff members began to exchange looks and feelings, for they all were thinking of all the possible things he could be talking about.

Brent pressed onward, and began to pace the room. While looking at the floor, he said, "My real name is David Webb. But, heh, you all already knew that."

Someone then sneezed; it sounded rather feminine. Brent, without looking up, said, "Bless you." He turned around and continued to pace the room. He then continued, "Now I want to know something, what do you all know about me, the real me, and why haven't any of you ever told me?" Brent paused, looked up, and studied all his staff.

They all looked at each other, and tried to silently decide who was going to talk. Eventually, S stood up from the couch and turned to Mrs. Green, whom was standing. "You can go ahead and take my seat, if you want," he told her very quietly, and very slowly, as per usual. "I don't plan on sitting back down." Mrs. Green then swiftly sat herself in S's seat. S then took a step forward, and towards Brent. He cleared his throat, and began his speech:

"Brent, I need to tell you something that we probably should have told you much earlier. Mrs. Bayer, Mrs. Green, and I were all very good friends of your parents, Mr. Claudio McIlrath, or should I say, Webb, and Mrs. Chondra Webb. We were all good friends, and knew each other quite well. We knew each other from just a stem of events that led us to our friendships. Digression aside, Brent, we all were just devastated when your parents died on that horrific fishing incident when you were just 18 years old. We couldn't stand by and see you suffer like that, but there wasn't really anything we could do at the time. We knew you quite well, through Claudio and Chondra, and you knew us quite well in return. After your parents died, you shut everyone out of your life except for, basically, Henry...er...Patrick. This went on for about two years. When you were 20 years old, you went on a camping trip with Patrick one weekend and never came back. A few days later, a few men from a company called Paradigm came to my door. I called over Mrs. Bayer and Mrs. Green; the men then told us about your lobotomy. We all were shocked, to say the least. They told us you were going to be given a new life, and that we were going to be a part of it. We all immediately said yes, even before we knew the terms and conditions; we figured this was what we could do to help you with your parent's absences.

"The men from Paradigm told us that your life was going to be given a new face, the whole being rich and everything else. They told us we were to be your 'servants' of sorts; maid, cook, and all-purpose caretaker. Those were the exact words they told us. So, then, we told them we would do it. We were also forced to sign an oath that says that we can never disclose this information to you…Well, you can see how well that worked out." S finally took a break in his long speech. It kind of tired him out, seeing as he was older and all.

Brent put his hand over his mouth and started to pace the room once more. He did so for a few moments, and looked at Mrs. Green and Mrs. Bayer. They're faces were pale, as if a ghost was standing in front of them. In a sense, there was.

"Who all doesn't know of my lobotomy, S?" Brent asked him, after he felt fit that S could muster up the answer.

"Well," S started. His eyes darted towards the ceiling as he called off the names, "Ms. Fisher, Mr. Nash, Mr. Rose, Ms. Laudinsky and Mr. Seitz. That's another story," S went on to say. "At first, it was only us three working for you. Eventually, we decided to start hiring some new people, the first being Mr. Nash. You liked him, we liked him; it was just a good fit. So, then you took it upon yourself to hire a few more people to take over playing 'guard' for the mansion. Then you added Mr. Rose, Ms. Laudinsky and Mr. Seitz to the list of workers. You also, if I remember, hired another maid before hiring Ms. Fisher; I can't remember her name, though." Brent shrugged his shoulders; he couldn't remember her name either. S continued, "Anyways, you fired her within a few weeks because, well, she was a bad worker. You didn't hire anyone else for a few years…and then one day you decided you wanted another maid, again. You put out the applications and you interviewed a few people, and then decided upon Ms. Fisher. Almost instantly, might I add."

"I remember that, S. Don't point it out to me…" Brent said, rather cold sounding.

"OK, well point being, only us three know about your…incident." S then finished his digressed story.

Brent paced around the room a bit more. Patrick just stood, leaning against a wall, trying to absorb everything being said. Eventually, Brent said, "OK," and drifted into silence once more. No one dared said anything until Brent asked them a direct question.

About three minutes passed until Brent spoke another word. "Patrick and I are leaving for Lawrence, Kansas tomorrow morning, and we might not be back for a few days. We're going to hopefully find out more about what happened to us." He paused and looked Mrs. Green, Mrs. Bayer, and S in their eyes. "You don't need to come in to work for a few days, if you want. I'll still pay you during my absence, don't worry. I only ask that Mr. Nash and all the other guards keep watch while I'm gone; I'm paranoid about that kind of stuff. I'll pass the word onto Ms. Fisher, too. Mrs. Bayer!" Her back straightened as she heard her name. Brent continued, "Go get Ms. Fisher and bring her in here, please. As for the rest of you, you may all leave now...goodbye."

Brent then turned his back. Everyone looked at one another, and eventually all got up and left. Mrs. Green and Mrs. Bayer went towards the faculty room, while S walked up towards Brent. He put his hand on his shoulder and only said, "Brent, I'm sorry. About everything." Brent opened his mouth to say something back, but words didn't come out. In S's eyes, he didn't see this; he just thought Brent was ignoring him. S then patted Brent's shoulder, and slowly walked out of the room, and towards the faculty room. Brent hung his head down low.

"Hey, uh," Patrick finally spoke words, "If it's no problem to you, I'm going to hit the hay early tonight. I see that you're in no real mood to talk about this right now, so I'll leave you be."

"That's fine, Patrick," Brent said, very solemnly. He added, "Good night," to his statement, as well. Patrick didn't reply, as he had already started to walk out of the room.

A few minutes of silence swept through the mansion. At some point, Hannah eventually walked into the living room, and she saw Brent staring towards the fireplace below the TV. "Um...Brent?" she asked.

Brent turned around to face her.

Hannah began to advance towards Brent. "Mrs. Bayer told me that you wanted to see me?"

"Yeah, I did," Brent said, trying to regain his composure. He should be used to this feeling, seeing as he's felt it a whole lot the past two days. Brent then went on, "I'm going to be going out of town for a few days, so you don't have to report to the mansion if you don't want to. You'll still get paid, don't worry."

"Alright, thanks," Hannah said, very breaking off. "Say, is everything alright with you? You don't seem like your normal self; at least, what I think is your normal self. I don't really know you all that well..."

"Huh?" Brent seemed to be caught off-guard by this. "No, I'm fine...It's just...listen, it doesn't concern you, alright? It's my problem, and I don't want you to get dragged into this, too."

"OK, I understand," Hannah said. She wasn't too entirely convinced, but she played along. She was more intrigued as to what he was referring to than anything. She reached into her pink bag and pulled out a little note pad. She dug around a bit more in the bag and eventually took out a pencil. She wrote down something on it, and tore off the paper from the pad and handed it to Brent. "Here's my phone number; in case you ever need to talk, or something."

"Thanks," Brent said back. He still sounded sad and depressed, but on the inside, he was screaming for joy. If Hannah wasn't here right now, he might have been celebrating, but that wasn't quite the case. He looked down at the paper, which read:

Hannah's phone number:
626-589-9932

Brent looked back up from the paper to see Hannah. Before he even realized it, she was around him; she hugged him. She then broke off the hug, and the two looked at each other awkwardly. Brent forced himself to let off a little smile, to show his appreciation.

"Well, I'm going to go now, Brent," she said.

"See ya," Brent said back. Hannah then left the room hesitantly, looking back at Brent every few seconds. Sooner than later, she disappeared. He then saw the other workers head for the door. He heard the front door open, and then shut almost as fast.

Brent was left standing in the living room, alone, with only his thoughts to keep him company. He was, at first, thinking about what S told him, but then he couldn't stop reliving the hug Hannah gave him. He was lost in a state of depression and happiness; , he didn't fall asleep easily that night.

Chapter 17

-Wait for Me; Rise Against-

The night made nothing visible. Darkness was all around. A man was walking forward, with no real intentions in mind. He only knew that if he walked forward for long enough, something good might come out of it. Besides, he figured it would be better to keep going forward than to sit there and do nothing. He heard grass being crushed underneath his feet as he walked; he assumed he must be in some sort of field.

Off in the distance, he saw a little light. He squinted his eyes to hopefully see it a little better, then began to walk a little faster. A light jog. A full-on sprint. Why was he running? He didn't know; his only intention was to see what this light was. As he grew closer to it, an outline of something started to form. It looked like a house. Once the man was within a few hundred feet of the shape, he verified that it was a house. A little problem with the house, though; it was on fire. Flames danced on top of the house, on the sides of the house, and around the base. The man then ran faster than he had before, and ran towards the house. As he approached the front porch, he heard a sound and stopped. Over the sounds of the blazing flames, he heard a distant, but still audible, "HELP!"

The man's adrenaline started to pump through his veins; he had to help whoever was stuck in this house. He approached the wooden door and tried opening the door via the doorknob; it was locked. "Of course..." the man said to himself, as he looked around, hoping to find some alternative to kicking down the door. No windows were nearby. He looked down and saw a Welcome mat. He picked it up and saw a key lying beneath it. There was only one problem with the key; it was shattered into two different pieces. The man placed the Welcome mat back down on the ground, seeing as he couldn't use the broken key for much of anything. The man then, not totally on board with the idea, took a few steps backward and revved himself up. He ran full-speed towards the door, shoulder first. He collided with the door with just enough force that the door swung open, and now the man was inside the house.

He looked around inside for a few moments. To his right were stairs that led to the 2nd floor. To his left was what looked to be like a living room. The ceiling was burning above him, as was basically everything else in the house. The man, trying to decide what to do next, heard a door slamming. It sounded to be coming from beyond the living room. The man rushed forward a little bit, and then turned to his right; he was now facing the kitchen. He looked around the kitchen and saw a door to his left. He ran toward it and opened it, hoping to find out why it suddenly shut. Maybe he would find someone here? Maybe they could tell him what's going on, or how the fire started?

When the man opened the door, he saw what seemed to be a field of some sort of crop. The man stepped out of the burning house for a moment and scanned the field, hoping to find something of significance. Off in the distance, he saw a silhouette of something running away. He couldn't make out any detail, and soon this darkened figure escaped the man's eyesight. The man's mind began to race, as multiple thoughts of what he just witnessed rushed into his consciousness. He wondered who could have left someone stranded in a burning house to die, while they ran off scot-free. He started to wonder how selfish someone would have to be to leave those that they care for, and make them suffer, because they're too scared of the matter at hand. These thoughts infuriated the man, but at the same time, he, too, thought of running away while he had the chance. Was it worth risking his life to save another's? Especially someone's whom he never knew; he didn't owe them anything.

While he was thinking this, he looked around the field once more, losing himself in his thoughts. Then he noticed something he hadn't seen before; off in the distance, he saw an American flag waving around at full-mast. Lights were positioned around the flag by its base, this way it was visible in the darkness of night. Seeing this, the man started to question his previous motives, and felt a sudden urge courage and determination rise from inside him; as if his only choice was to save this mysterious person's life from this burning building. Not because he had to, but because he wanted to; he felt it was the right thing to do. After rethinking his current actions, the man turned around to enter the burning house once more.

Entering the kitchen, the man thought of using an oven mitt to open any door that might be potentially hot while searching for this person inside of the house. While he was searching, he heard another cry for help; it sounded like it was coming from upstairs. The man soon found an oven mitt, and headed directly for the upstairs; he didn't waste his time looking in the doors that were on the main floor. While walking out of the kitchen, the man heard a loud, "CRACK!" from above him. He ducked and rushed forward, and behind him a large plank of burning wood crashed into the floor; the same space he was standing in a few moments ago. Had he have been standing there, he most likely would have been dead. The man decided to be more cautious from here on out.

After carefully making his way towards the stairs, the man looked towards the 2nd floor to see what was ahead of him. On the stairs were a few planks of burning wood randomly thrown about, as well as a few patches of missing floor. Dodging the dangers with grace, the man made his way up the stairs; he also noticed how hot and tired he was becoming. Another "HELP!" was screamed from what seemed to be his left-side; he didn't even bother checking the one door to his right.

The man checked every single door on his left; he used the oven mitt to open all of them. The rooms he saw were vaguely familiar to him; he seemed to know where everything was in the rooms once he saw them. The first room he checked looked to be a kid's room; the walls were painted gold and there were posters of rock bands everywhere, all of them on fire. The heat from the fire everywhere started to get to the man; he began to sweat more than he ever had before in his life, and was beginning to grow even more tired.

The next room he checked was a bathroom. He didn't spend too much time in here, for it was very warm in there. Oddly enough, no fire was in this room. The man looked very quickly at the mirror that was hung next to the door. The man saw his reflection, but at the same time not really. His face and body was charred-looking, and covered in soot (or that's what he assumed it was, at least). He quickly left the bathroom and proceeded to open the next door; the last door he could check. Before opening it, he hesitated for some reason. He, once more, started to question his motives and started to wonder if this was all worth it to save the life of someone he didn't even know. Was it worth everything the man had to do what he thought was right?

He stood outside the door sweating and hyperventilating, fire all around him, hearing wood crashing into the foundation of the house; he didn't have much longer until the house totally collapsed. "HELP!" was screamed once more, now much louder and blood curling that ever had been before. The man then was taken out of his daze, and decided to stop procrastinating and proceeded to try and open the door. As he put the mitt on the door and turned, he realized how tired he suddenly became; he was using most of the energy he had left to even turn the doorknob. How was he going to help someone out of this burning house if he could hardly even open the door to the room this person was trapped in?

The doorknob turned, and the door pushed open. A rush of cooler air came over the man; he felt a little more energy being supplied to him. He walked into the room and suddenly all colors faded to a monotonic black and gray color as the sudden burst of energy he had just felt left him, and his movements became much slower. His eyes began to strain and his head hurt beyond all belief. His eyelids were like weights to hold up, and the man felt like he was about to pass out. Almost about to collapse, the man noticed that he was in a baby's room. The walls had a very infant-theme to it, and baby powder, baby toys, and other baby things were all around the room as well. The man noticed a little bit of movement coming from the baby crib in front of him, so he moved towards it with all his remaining energy.

He looked inside of the crib to see possibly the weirdest and creepiest thing on God's green Earth. In the crib was a young child, one who looked to be a little too old to be in a baby crib. Its body was outlined by darkness, and only its face was visible. "HELP!" it screamed out. Once it was done with its cry, the child's neck cricked itself in a way that was painful to watch, and it began to mutter to itself, "Why'd he leave...why'd he leave..." Its voice, however, sounded like the man's own voice, although a little slower. The child must have felt the man's presence, as it cricked its neck towards him and then quietly said, "Please don't leave me...I need you." The man was freaked out, and did not want to be anywhere near this thing. He was also beginning to think this could just be his tired mind playing games with him, and that's he's just seeing things. He figured that's the most likely of solutions, but was still spooked all the same.

Amid his confusion, the floor beneath the man started to rumble, as did the rest of the house, it seemed. The man froze in his place out of fear, and within moments the man fell through the floor, along with the child, and the ceiling above both. The man hit the main floor, and he felt an immense pain shoot through his legs. He screamed out in such agony that anyone within a mile radius would have heard him. It didn't last long, though; the burning wood from the ceiling above fell on top of him. He felt a large piece of the wood begin to break the surface of his skull. The man's scream was cut short, and soon all pain was relieved from him...

The house collapsed.

Chapter 18

-Key Entity Extraction V: Sentry the Defiant; Coheed and Cambria-

The next morning, Brent and Patrick began to pack up their things, for they were soon leaving for Lawrence, Kansas. Patrick is bringing along all his belongings, basically. He has with him all that he brought to the mansion, and whatever he had in his dumpster (Brent is going to stop by there on their way out and pick up his things-assuming they're still there). Brent, on the other hand, is bringing along some clothes for both Brent and Patrick to wear while in Lawrence. He also has his cell phone, a charger for the phone, his wallet, and lastly the picture of him and his parents that sits on his bedside. He slipped this in at the last minute, and it was unbeknownst to Patrick.

Brent, before leaving the mansion, called up a hotel in Lawrence, Kansas, and made reservations for a room. It was surprisingly easy; Patrick was almost certain that it would be much harder than it really was. Anyways, Brent made the reservations and that was that.

Once the two were ready to leave, they walked down into the lobby of the mansion. It was weird seeing the mansion so empty, Brent thought. Usually his workers get shorter hours on weekends, but they're at least there in the morning and stay until lunch. Brent also got the chance to notice how much their footsteps echoed in the lobby; he never really noticed that before, oddly. After walking through the lobby, the two walked towards the parking garage, and Brent and Patrick got into Brent's car and drove off.

Before making progress towards Lawrence, Kansas, Brent made a couple stops. One was to Patrick's dumpster which he used to call home. (Brent and Patrick made an agreement that morning; no matter what happens in Lawrence, Patrick will stay at the mansion until he can get back to supporting himself on his own.) Patrick got out of the car and nabbed his things, for they were all there, surprisingly. When he got back in the car, he kept his albums in the front seat, and he threw his blanket and pillow in the back seat. Brent then got out of the car himself and disposed of the dirty blanket and pillow. "Yeah, probably not a good idea to keep them, huh?" Patrick said whenever Brent got back in the car; Brent just shook his head sarcastically and drove on.

The second stop was a short one; Brent stopped by the music store to pick up his New Medicine CD that he reserved a few days ago. When he walked in to pick it up, the woman working the front desk asked him, "Why'd ya wait so long to pick up your album, sir?"

"Long story short, I got busy," Brent replied to her. The conversation then died and he got his album. He popped it in as soon as he got in the car, and that marked the beginning of the two's journey to Lawrence, Kansas.

For most of the five-hour car ride there, the two didn't talk much. They just listened to a lot of music. Most of which being a lot of Rise Against, Coheed and Cambria, Stone Sour, Anthrax, and of course the newest New Medicine CD. At a certain point, however, Patrick couldn't stay silent any longer. He said, breaking tension, "Hey, Brent, listen, I'm sorry about ditching you last night. Well, that and I'm sorry about the whole situation last night, really."

"It's fine," Brent replied. He turned down the music to a low murmur. "I kind of wasn't in the mood to really talk about it last night, anyways. Plus, I went to bed not too long after you did. Did I fall asleep relatively quickly, though? No, not even close." Brent took his eyes off the road and looked at Patrick for a second. Patrick looked like a little kid when he was confessing that he ate the last piece of cake to his parents. He then put his eyes back on the road. "Know what, though? I'm glad I talked to them about it; it helped relieve some stress from my mind, in a way. Plus, we know some more information now; Paradigm is what this company is called." Brent paused and said under his breath, "The name does kinda ring a bell..." Patrick, however, did not hear that last bit.

"Well do you want to talk about any of it?" Patrick asked.

"What is there to say?" Brent replied. "I mean, they took over in my parents' place once I-I mean, we were lobotomized. I'm glad they did; who knows what might have happened if they decided to be assholes to me like I was to them, and they didn't step in and help out." Brent paused. "And, I guess the more I think about it, it is a little weird to think that I can recall the moment that they claim I started my new life. It's even weirder to think that my fake memories go even before that. It's all just...I don't know." Brent came to a stop at a stop light. He took this time to answer Patrick directly to his face. He went on, "It's just hard to talk about, you know? Like, the words are there but I just can't formulate anything out of them. It's weird."

"I get ya," Patrick said back. He understood the feeling; that was practically him in a nutshell for the past few days. Patrick sensed that Brent just wasn't in the mood to talk about it, so he let off and changed the subject. "So...what happened with you and Hannah last night, huh?"

The car began to move again. "Uh..." Brent said back to him. He was trying to think up a clever way to reply to Patrick; he didn't really feel like hearing a, "K-I-S-S-I-N-G" chant for the rest of the trip. "Nothing. I just called her in, and I told her that she didn't have to report to work for a few days cause I'd-we'd be out of town."

"And then...?" Patrick suggested.

"Dammit, he's not letting off..." Brent thought. Patrick kind of had him beat, so he just bit the bullet: "Then she gave me her phone number and hugged me. That's it, OK?"

Patrick couldn't hide the smile on his face if he was standing behind a mountain. "Dude, you are so fucking money," he said.

"What?"

"You are so fucking money, and you don't even know it, baby!"

Brent finally caught on to the reference.

"OK, Trent, you can lay off it now. It's done, it's over. So, let's just drop it." Brent told him. Patrick just let out a sort of maniacal laugh; Brent became scared for what else Patrick could/would say for the rest of the trip.

The two grew quiet for a few moments. Patrick then whispered, "So fucking money, man..."

"Quiet," Brent commanded. Patrick began to laugh again, but this time not as maniacal. The two never really talked again after that, so Brent soon turned the music back up in his car. Brent and Patrick both seemed to be in a better mood after their talk; it was nice to finally clear the air with one another. Sometimes that just needs to be done...

They only really talked two other times on that trip; the first being when they were at lunch, where they stopped off at a Burger King. There they just talked about College Basketball, because the two used to be big about that back when they were in High School...well, at least that's what their memories told them.

The other time they talked was in the carried, about an hour before reaching their hotel. Brent was driving down a long, straight road with no other cars around, and Patrick said, "Hey, do you know how much longer we have 'til we're in Lawrence?"

"I don't know, maybe another hour or so?"

"You mind if we turn back?"

Brent glared over at Patrick and said, "Now why in the hell would we turn back? Did you leave the oven running?"

"No...smartass...I just...I don't know."

Brent pulled over to the side of the road and put the car in park. He turned and said, "Patrick, is there something wrong? What's going on?"

"Nothing," he replied, "I just...I don't really want to find out any more about us, you know? I mean, we've already found out so much, and who really cares who we were in our past lives?"

"I care who we were," Brent retorted. "Just as you should. How could you not want to see what this whole, 'Paradigm' business is all about?"

Patrick closed his eyes, looked down at the floorboard and released, "Because, frankly, I'm scared. I don't want to find out anymore because I'm scared to know what the answer is." He looked up and looked at Brent. "I mean, what if we were horrible axe murderers, or child rapists? I'd just rather live in doubt wondering what my past life was than know a horrifying truth, and then have to live with it until I die."

Brent sympathized with Patrick, "Dude, I'm scared too. How could either of us not be scared? Cause, like you said what if we are axe murderers? You think I want to drive 5 hours out of my way just to find out we were murderers, and lobotomies were our form of punishment?" He said this with some form of sarcasm to it.

"That's another thing, though," Patrick went on, "What if when we're in Lawrence we never find out anything? What if Chris is just this insane nut job that doesn't know anything about our pasts? If that's the case then we would have gained nothing from all this! We could have just stayed in Preston and maybe asked Ken or Jaime about more info."

Brent's face scrunched up when he heard Jaime. He remembered that they might have had to do something with him, but he couldn't remember exactly what...he quickly disregarded this thought.

Brent responded to Patrick's fears with, "That could be true; we could get in Lawrence, ask Chris about this, and not find out jack shit. But I must know the answer to this. I'd rather we go and ask Chris and learn nothing than sit at home with our thumbs up our asses, hoping that Ken or Jesse will squeal about what they did to us."

Patrick bit his lip and his eyes looked around the inside of the car.

Brent continued, "Patrick, I think we actually know more about what happened to us than we think we do. I think we're more than halfway to finding out the truth about our pasts...we just need triggers."

"Triggers?"

"Yeah, triggers. You know, like when Ken said Henry and you remembered all these memories suddenly for no reason? That's what I'm hoping to find in Lawrence, triggers; triggers to activate our memories again."

Brent grew quiet, and Patrick thought for a few moments before saying, "You're making a lot of sense, Brent…"

"I know I am," Brent said, with a little bit of cockiness in his voice. Patrick smiled. "But if you're not going to go through with this for yourself, at least go through with this for me."

Patrick looked down at the floorboard again, and said in a sigh, "I can't argue that. I can give up on myself all I want, but what kind of person would I be if I gave up, and it affected those around me."

"So, we're still going to Lawrence, then?" Brent asked.

Patrick looked up and said very agitated, "Yes. We're going to Lawrence…"

Brent chuckled at this and drove up onto the road once more and continued driving towards their hotel.

About 20 minutes before reaching their hotel, Brent suddenly saw these bright blue and red lights that looked to be coming from behind them. Patrick became curious, along with Brent, and the two looked in the rear-view mirror. What they saw was a police car.

"Crap," Brent said. "We were so close, too." Brent looked down at his speedometer, which read "75 mph."

Brent pulled over, and effectively turned off the music in the car. He turned to Patrick and said, "Not to sound like a dick or anything, but please don't say anything to the officer. I don't want to be here any longer than I have to."

"We're in the same boat, buddy," Patrick agreed.

After a few minutes of waiting, Brent heard a tapping on his window. He rolled down the window and looked out to see a police woman bending down next to his car. She was wearing a standard police uniform: black shirt, black pants, gun holster, badge, etc. She was rather short, skinny too; neither of which added much to her intimidation factor. She was wearing sunglasses, and her long-ish brown hair was in a ponytail. This made her look more like an average person, and less like a big scary cop.

"Hello, officer," Brent said in a very calm, casual voice, "What seems to be the problem?"

"Well, for one you were going 75 in a 50 zone," she began, "But before we talk about that, does your name happen to be David Webb?"

"Uhh..." Brent didn't know how to answer that. He glanced over to Patrick, hoping that he could help in some way. He looked just about as horrified as Brent was. Brent then decided to say, "Yes, I am. Why does it matter to you-uh, ma'am?"

"Really? You don't recognize me?" The female officer then took her sunglasses off and messed with her hair a little bit. Doing this revealed her brown eyes, and Brent also noticed a few freckles on her face. She was starting to look more familiar to him. "I'm Jenna. Jenna Smith, remember? We went to High School together."

Memories started to rush back through both Brent and Patrick's heads as they suddenly realized who they were talking to. "Oh my God," Brent said, with his mouth wide open, "Yes, I remember you now! Wow, it's been so long!"

"Yeah, I know," Jenna said. "I graduated when you were still a sophomore. Wow, that was such a long time ago...time flies, huh?"

"Yeah," Brent said with a little nervous laugh, "Trust me, I know all about that."

"Who's in the car with you?" Jenna asked Brent, as she leaned her head into the car a little more. "Oh, is that Henry?"

"The one and only," Patrick replied with a little cockiness.

"Hi Henry!" Jenna exclaimed. "Sorry I didn't see you earlier, or I would have said something."

"Nah it's cool," Patrick said back.

Jenna took her head out of the car, but still near Brent's head. "So how have you two been doing these past few years, huh?" she asked.

"Fine, I guess," Brent answered.

"I agree with what David said," Patrick said.

"Well that's cool...I guess," Jenna said, not totally satisfied with their answers. She went on, "I've been doing pretty good! I'm a police officer now, as you can see. Well, not really a police officer as I am a traffic cop, but whatever." She started to get a little nervous for some reason; she took her eyes off Brent and Patrick and tried to make little eye contact with them. "I'm currently living with my boyfriend, Sam Hill, too!" She waited for a reply from either Brent or Patrick, but she received none. She seemed annoyed by this, "You know; my boyfriend from High School."

"Oh, yes, him! Congratulations!" Brent said. Neither Brent nor Patrick remembered who this "Sam Hill" character was, but they played along with it; they figured it's probably easier this way. "So, go on, tell me more," Brent added, not wanting to sound rude.

"Well anyway, yeah, we're living together now. We've been doing this for...oh, I'd say six years now. He moved to Lawrence for job-related issues, and he asked me to go with him and we could live together. I agreed almost instantly!"

Patrick leaned closer to where Jenna was standing outside of the car and said, "So are you two married yet, or what?"

"No, not yet," Jenna replied sadly. "Every time we go out, I keep expecting him to get down on a knee and propose, but alas not yet. He's always been shy with things...I mean, we went out for a year before we even held hands! You two remember that story, right?" Brent and Patrick shook their heads like they knew what she was talking about. They didn't. Jenna continued, "We're going out for a fancy dinner tonight, so," Jenna crossed her fingers, "Here's hoping he proposes! Then again, I've been saying the same thing for a long time now." The group then received a few moments of awkward silence. Jenna then broke that silence, "So what are you two doing in Lawrence, Kansas? It's quite a distance from Preston, Oklahoma."

"We're, uh..." Brent broke off so he could try and think up a good lie.

Patrick, however, finished Brent's sentence. "We're here just to walk around. I've always said that I wanted to go to Lawrence, and my good friend, David, here," he put his hand on Brent's shoulder, "said he'd take me if I would just shut up about it."

"Well that's a very nice thing to do, David," Jenna said to him.

"Yeah, his girlfriend is at home, because she didn't want to go with us." Patrick casually threw that in, because he knew it would just piss off Brent.

"Ooh, David has a new girlfriend now?" Jenna said, in an almost teasing-like tone.

"*I hate you so much right now, Patrick,*" Brent thought.

Jenna went on, "So what's her name? That's all I want to know!"

Brent refused to answer; too bad he's friends with Patrick. Patrick answered for him, "Her name's Hannah Fisher. She's quite the cutie!"

"Aww, that's sweet! Send me pics of you two sometime, OK?"

Brent just sat there, staring forward, looking more aggravated. He began to tap his fingers on the steering wheel. "I'll be sure that he sends them to you," Patrick answered for him, once more.

"Cool." Jenna then started to act more serious. "OK, well I still have to do my job, unfortunately. So, I'm going to need to see your license and registration, please."

"Oh, yeah, sure," Brent said. He then dug into his back pocket for his wallet and pulled out his license. He handed it to Jenna, and as soon as he let go of the license, he realized that he had just made a horrible mistake.

"Hey, um, David," Jenna said, "Why does it say Brent McIlrath on your license?"

"*Dammit!*" Brent and Patrick both thought. The two then knew they couldn't get out of this one, and they just told Jenna their entire story, including what new information they learned last night.

"Oh wow," Jenna said after the two were finally done telling their story to her. "Uh, I'm, wow…I'm sorry to hear about all that."

"It's OK, it's not your fault; you didn't know," Brent said. "Actually, no one knows."

Jenna smiled a little at that. She then asked, "Are you two sure, though, that this is all true? Because, no offense, but it's kind of hard to believe this farfetched of a story. Plus, I'm a little confused about all this..."

Brent and Patrick showed her their heads, with the flower-shaped scars on them. Brent looked up and said, "These designs are our lobotomy scars; we both have them, and both Ken and Jaime said they are from the lobotomy."

Jenna still looked a bit skeptical, and said, "There are still some things that don't stack up, though..."

Patrick cut her off; "Trust us, we know. That's the real reason why we're here in Lawrence; to try and get more pieces to this puzzle." Jenna seemed satisfied by this, for she never asked any more questions. Patrick then asked her, "Just a quick question, though, have you ever heard of that company we mentioned, Paradigm?"

"No, never, until now," Jenna replied. "In fact, I don't think I'll be of much real help to you guys. All I know is what you told me...I'm sorry."

"It's fine; it's OK," Brent said, trying to reassure Jenna.

"Here, here's something that might help you two out." Jenna handed back Brent's license. "I'm going to act like your speeding incident never happened, OK?"

"Wow, thanks!" Brent exclaimed.

"Plus, I'll give you a police escort to your hotel. Where are you two headed?" Brent told her. "OK, that works out perfectly! My shift's over now and the station is on the way there. You two just hang tight here for a few moments; when I get ahead of you two and turn on my lights, start following behind me." She then put her sunglasses back on and walked towards her police car. Brent and Patrick followed her instructions, and soon they were given a police escort to their hotel. They, in all honesty, probably didn't need the escort, but they appreciated the help nonetheless.

Once Jenna had successfully led Brent and Patrick to their hotel, Jenna parked her car, as did Brent, and got out.

She walked up towards Brent's window; he rolled it down. "There ya go, you two!"

"Thanks again, Jenna," Brent said in response.

"No problem. Hey, good luck with your search; both of you. If you need any help, just go down to the police station," Jenna pointed to her left, "in that direction, about a mile or so down, and ask for Jenna. They'll contact me, and I'll do my best to help."

Patrick leaned over and said, "I don't think that will be necessary, but we'll keep that in mind regardless."

"Well good!" Jenna said back with a little more charisma. "I'll be on my way then. Nice getting to see you two again; bye!"

"See ya," Brent said as Jenna began to walk away from the car. "Wait!" he yelled suddenly. "Would you happen to still be in contact with Chris?"

Jenna turned around and got up next to the car door again and said, "Kind of. We don't talk much, anymore; he kinda went off the deep end of loony-vile, talking about brain washing, or something…huh…maybe he's linked to this somehow?"

"That's what our money's on," Brent finished. "Well, thank you again, Jenna."

"Don't mention it," she said as she walked away and got in her own car and drove off towards the direction that she said the police station was.

Brent then turned to Patrick, "Ready to go check in?"

"Yeah, I guess," he replied. "Say, what time is it? I'm starving."

Brent turned the key in the car so that the radio would turn on. "About 6PM…" Brent then realized how hungry he was too. "OK, let's just go check in, drop off our things, and then I'll go to a local pizza joint; it's really good."

"Sounds good to me," Patrick said as he started to undo his seatbelt. Brent did the same, and the two then grabbed their things from all-about the car and walked into the hotel lobby.

The lobby looked rather well-kept; the walls were spotless, as were the carpeted floors; the wallpaper matched up with the green colored carpet, too. A lone table with a fish in a bowl sat next to the entrance. Patrick thought that was a rather weird spot to put a fish, but whatever. The two walked up towards the main desk, where a man with glasses stood with his back hunched over some piece of paper.

"Hello," Brent said to the man as he approached the desk.

The man looked up and said, in a friendly, energetic tone, "Hello there! Welcome to LaQuinta Inn! How may I help you two fine gentlemen?"

Brent really wasn't expecting such kindness out of the worker, but he pressed on. "Um, I made reservations to here this morning; we're here to check into our room."

"Certainly, sir! What might be your name?"

"Brent McIlrath."

"OK..." the man then turned the computer that was nearest to him and started to type. "Uh, what did you say your last name was again?"

"McIlrath. M-C-I-L-R-A-T-H," Brent spelled out.

"Thank you," the man whispered as he typed the name into the computer. "Yup, you certainly did make reservations!" He then walked back over to the paper he was looking at when the two-walked in. He grabbed a pen and asked, "Is room number 588 good for you two?"

"I don't see why it wouldn't be," Brent replied, trying to act comical. The worker didn't seem to get it.

"OK then!" exclaimed the worker, "I'll put you down for room 588 then. Just take the elevator behind you up to floor 5. It should be the second-to-last door on the right side. If I remember correctly, it's near the stairs." The man then gave Brent the key to his room; it wasn't a credit card-looking thing like most other room keys. It was an actual key, which Brent thought was a little odd.

"Alright, thank you," Brent said to the worker. He then put the room key into his pocket. The worker started to write down Brent's name on the paper as the two took themselves and their things up to their room.

They followed the worker's instructions as to where the room was, and they soon found their room. Brent pulled out the room key from his pocket and stuck it into the keyhole. "CLICK." The door opened.

The hotel room looked like any other normal hotel room. The carpet had a weird floral design to them, the wallpaper was also bland. The bathroom was to their immediate left as they entered the room; it was small and dainty, but then again, this was a hotel bathroom. Directly in front of them was their beds; two twin size beds, just as Brent had asked for. Facing the beds was their small box-shaped TV, which only picked up the local news stations. Not like they planned on watching the newest episode of, "Dance Moms" anyway. The two dropped off their belongings into the room and made a beeline directly to the car, for they were very hungry.

Upon getting back in the car, and turning on the ignition, Patrick looked at the clock: 6:15PM.

"How is it this late already? It's only, like, a five-hour drive from Preston to Lawrence," Patrick said, sounding a little frustrated.

"Well, we did take a few pit stops along the way. Plus, we talked with Jenna for a while," Brent replied, trying to bring rationality into this.

"Yeah, I guess that makes sense." Patrick then asked, "How far away is this pizza place?"

Brent pulled out of the parking lot. "About 5 minutes from here. Don't worry, they're fast there."

"They better be…" Patrick said quietly. He becomes a little grumpy when he's hungry.

In due time, the two had made it to the place that Brent was talking about, Morningstar Pizza. The place itself was rather small, and kind of congested. The service was more of a, "get in, get out ASAP" type deal, which was fine for both Brent and Patrick. They didn't really feel like waiting forever to get their food. Morningstar was rather unique in it that you didn't necessarily order a pizza, but more you ordered slices of a pizza. But damn are they huge slices. Once slice should be good enough to feed one person and then some! Brent and Patrick ate quickly because of their hunger, and were in and out of the place in about 10 minutes.

At this point, the two decided to do a little walking around in Lawrence, Kansas. They stopped by a local bookstore, and look around at all the Kansas Jayhawk material; the two were very big KU fans. They stole a few lanyards and dog tags (they were free, so saying they stole them is going a bit overboard) from the bookstore, and looked at all the shirts the store had to offer. It also had a few other goodies in it as well, like KU blankets, KU tents, water bottles, backpacks, folders, etc. Once they looked at everything they could look at, the left the store. Outside of the bookstore, they noticed, was a statue that looked like the Kansas Jayhawk and a mermaid did the fusion dance, and gave birth to a monstrosity.

Their next stop that night, and the last one they did for that day, was they went to the actual Kansas University and looked at the Hall of Fame in the Allen Fieldhouse. They didn't say for very long, but they got to look at all the rings and awards that KU won so far in its existence.

"Man, I remember when I was little," Brent recollected, "I, my mother, and my father all came down to Lawrence for a weekend. We came down to watch a KU basketball game. If I recall correctly, I think they won that game by a landslide. Before the game, we walked around the town, looked in all the shops, explored the actual university a little…I remember having a great time! I wish I could go back to then…" Brent broke off and said no more of it; he started to recall more and more of that trip, but he kept it inside of his head. Patrick didn't say anything; he just absorbed what Brent was telling him. He felt it more respectful that way.

After leaving Allen Fieldhouse, Brent and Patrick decided to get back to the hotel and rest up, for tomorrow was going to be a big day for the two of them. When they got back to the hotel, they turned on the lights and changed into their nighttime clothing. Brent, upon getting ready for bed, realized that he hadn't packed a toothbrush or toothpaste for either of them. *"Dammit…"* Brent thought to himself as he realized this. He then just figured the two wouldn't brush their teeth for a while, which sounded disgusting but wasn't as bad as he thought it would be.

As the two began to settle in their separate beds, Brent turned on the TV and decided to watch the news a little before heading off to bed. The TV was tuned into Channel 2, so the Channel 2 news was on. On the corner of the screen, the two saw that the time was 8:43PM.

"Holy crap, I didn't realize that we were out that long," Patrick thought aloud.

"I know, right," Brent said back. The two then quieted down and watched the news, and saw what it had to offer. They were in for more than just the local news, the two found out.

"...so, it will be a little windy tomorrow, wind chill at 46 degrees F. Bring a jacket with you; the sun might be shining, but that doesn't mean it will make the air any warmer!" The meteorologist was on; he was a little pudgy, and he wore a blue suit. He was waving his hands in front of the green screen, predicting the weather for all to see.

"Alright, thank you, Kent," the anchorwoman said, transitioning into her section. She had her hair short, brown, and she wore a bright red suit, which was kind of distracting. "Well, two interesting stores have just been given to us, both from a little town called Preston, Oklahoma."

Brent and Patrick didn't say anything to each other; they both watched attentively, hoping it wouldn't be them in the newscast.

The anchorwoman went on, "A wanted man for date rape, by the name of Guy Lawrence..." a picture of the creepy man that Brent and Patrick saw from the bar two nights ago was displayed in the right-hand corner of the screen.

"Hey, hey!" Patrick burst out, "That's the guy who was arrested at that bar!"

The newscast continued, "...was arrested two nights ago at a local Preston, Oklahoma bar. He was arrested by Officer Colton, who gives his account of what happened."

The focus then shifted from the anchorwoman to a camera, in which an interview with this police officer was shown. Officer Colton looked rather muscular, and about in his mid-30s. He had orange hair, and no facial hair to speak off. His voice had a bit of deepness to it, but also with a hint of a southern accent. He was quoted with saying, "…yeah, I was just sitting there, enjoying a drink, going to watch a local band, when I saw Guy walk in. I know exactly who he was the minute I first laid eyes on his ugly mug. At that point, I tried to stay hidden from him, so that I could catch him in the act. Eventually, he did it [tried to drug-up a girl], and I caught him. Not much more to say about that…"

Now the anchorwoman was back on screen. "The other story is that of an almost murder and a suicide." Brent and Patrick both let off a sigh of relief, but also one of great concern. They were off the hook, but they were also concerned about there being a murder-suicide in their hometown. The anchorwoman continued by saying, "27-year-old Jaime Belcher…" A picture of Jaime was put up in the right-hand corner of the screen. Brent and Patrick both put their hands in front of their mouths in unison. "…shot and almost killed his pregnant wife, Acacia Belcher, then turned the gun on himself. We have an audio-only interview with Acacia with a few more details."

A screen with a tape recorder and subtitles of what Acacia was saying was displayed on the screen now. "…he came home looking like a mess. I asked what was wrong, and he didn't answer. I asked again, and he said, 'I don't know anymore.' I thought it to be a rather odd answer, but I was working on dinner at that time, so I continued with what I was doing. Later, I called him down for dinner when it was ready, and he emerged in the kitchen with a gun in his hands, and he shot me right above my breast. I started to fall back, and I didn't see what happened next, but I heard another gunshot. It wasn't until later I found out he killed himself. I passed out almost immediately after I was shot, and my next memory was me waking up in the hospital…"

The screen then showed the anchorwoman again, who went on, "And as if that wasn't enough, the sadistic man was recording the entire act with a camera, and the whole scene was captured on tape. We are not allowed to show it on television, and that might probably be for the best. We are being told that Acacia is in stable condition, and that the baby is still alive and won't be affected any from this incident-" Brent shut off the TV.

"Wow..." Patrick uttered. He hung his head low.

"I just can't believe it," Brent said, "Jaime...oh God, Jaime, how could you...?"

"That's just..." Patrick stopped. He couldn't think of the words to describe what he wanted to say. "He shouldn't have done it," he finally said.

"He was just such an upbeat guy, or at least that's what he was in my memories. He shouldn't have gone out of this world like this...even if he did lobotomize us." Brent looked to Patrick. "I wonder if us showing up again changed him...maybe...maybe we're the reason that he's dead, in a way?" Patrick looked up at Brent, with a puzzled look on his face. Brent continued, "Well, I mean, he didn't seem to be in the right state of mind when we left him a few days ago in his office. So, you know, maybe we're the reason that he killed himself, and his wife. We reminded him of a guilt that was too difficult for him to bear..."

"To be honest with you, Brent," Patrick said quietly, "I wouldn't doubt that."

The room grew quiet, and Brent suddenly jumped up and blurted out, "Oh shit! We were supposed to meet with Jaime yesterday!" Patrick suddenly remembered too, and his eyes widened at the realization. Meanwhile, Brent still spoke, "Arg, maybe if we saw him then maybe he wouldn't be dead...Stupid, stupid, STUPID!" He began to hit his face with his palm.

"Hey, hey," Patrick said, trying to calm him down, "That could be true, but that might also not be true. He probably died a few days ago, so seeing him yesterday wouldn't have amounted to anything."

Brent stopped hitting himself. "That's supposed to make me feel better?"

"I'm just saying' is all."

Brent hung his head down low. "God, I just feel like this is all my fault..."

"It's not your fault," Patrick told him, "If anything, it's our fault, but it isn't that. We could do anything to prevent this."

"We could have not showed up to his shop Thursday."

"Well, yeah, but then where would we be?" Patrick said forcefully. Brent grew quiet. "Exactly. Now let's just go to bed. We have a long day tomorrow and we need the rest." Brent agreed, but before going to bed completely, the two, while not being very religious of people, said a short prayer for Jaime, Acacia, and their unborn child. They felt guilty about the situation, even if they might have not had any direct affiliation of Jaime's heinous act. Even if Jaime shouldn't be prayed for, given what he did to get himself out of this world, the two still felt as if this was the right thing to do. They both fought to hold back tears, for they knew if they started to cry they wouldn't be able to stop.

Late on into the night, Brent sat awake in bed. He couldn't stop thinking about everything that has transpired in the past few days, as well as his thoughts on Hannah, and the news they learned that night about Jaime. He had almost a feeling of guilt for some of it, but at the same time, he felt like none of it was his fault. As he was having this mental war, he looked over to his left and tried to see if Patrick was asleep. He couldn't really see anything, for it was so dark, but he heard the deep and slowed breathing coming from Patrick; he assumed that he was asleep from that. Brent reached over to the nightstand that divided the two beds from each other, and grabbed his phone from its charging cord. He checked the time: 10:10PM. He laid the phone back down and rolled back over, trying to fall asleep once more. Outside of the room, Brent heard someone walking in, what he recognized to be, high heels. He heard the noise travel past his room's door, and a loud noise came from the door next to his room; room 589. It sounded almost like the person collided with the door. He heard this person say, "Shit!" in a very feminine voice. Brent recognized this voice, and he knew who it was! He wanted to spring out of his bed and open the door to see them, but he was too inflicted with fear to do so. As he sat there longer, he heard the person fiddling with what sounded like keys, and he heard this person drop the keys onto the floor. "Really?" he heard this mysterious woman say. Brent could verify that he knew who this was now. Again, the feeling to spring out of his bed came over him, but even quicker than before he was shot down by his own cowardice. Instead he sat there and listened to the person eventually open the door to her room and walk in. The door slammed behind her. Brent sat there in silence once more, trying to fall asleep.

Sleep didn't come so easily to Brent that night, though.

Made in the USA
Monee, IL
08 January 2022

88434056R00111